SONGS OF PASSION

SONGS *of* PASSION

NAMIAR TOPIT

Content Warning

This book contains themes that might not be suitable for all audiences.
Including but not limited to:

Transphobia, violence, profanity, morally grey main characters, nudity, explicit and rough sex, BDSM (rope bondage, submission, dominance).

ISBN 978-952-65138-0-5 (Paperback)
ISBN 978-952-65138-1-2 (Hardcover)
ISBN 978-952-65138-2-9 (EPUB)

Edited by KG Brightwell

For Iina
Thank you for all the coffee and tea therapy it took to write this

SIREN'S CALL

It was safe to say I absolutely *detested* weddings. There was nothing more nauseating than having to attend them. Sitting in a non-ergonomic chair for at least an hour, often while mentally suffocating. Most likely in a religious establishment too, chosen by the main stars of the day. Listening to two people swearing eternal love, only to find them in the divorce statistics a few years later.

Weddings—they always went in similar cookie-cutter fashion, especially the ceremony. Even this lesbian one, despite having been promised it wouldn't be as stiff and formal as a regular wedding. Having been raised Catholic, I'd developed the skill to sit through pretty much anything, though, so I took a deep breath to brace myself.

We were all seated on a huge LA mansion's terrace, looking at the overly ornate wedding arch facing the glimmering ocean, sweating under the glaring West Coast sun in the previously mentioned uncomfortable chairs that were arranged in a similar fashion to a typical church. Truthfully, I hadn't spotted much of a difference, except the obvious lack of religion.

This difference was certainly not enough to stop the kids crying because of ultimate boredom—and honestly, all adults wanted to throw tantrums as well but lacked the courage the kids had. The absence of religious content clearly didn't stop Aunt Becky—there was always an Aunt Becky—from developing a lung disease a minute before the music started. She sounded like a dying behemoth as she tried to somehow manage to cough inwardly.

Everyone seemed to collectively decide to not stare, but failed magnificently, until finally a lady in green three rows down from Aunt Becky handed over a pack of mints to the lady in red sitting in front of her.

"Here, can you pass it forward?" she said, and leaned back, with a content smile briefly caressing her lips as if she'd done her mandatory good deed of the day.

I watched the pack of mints reach Aunt Becky with mild curiosity. Once they did, she apologized and thanked everyone profusely, nodding so much that her dirty blond helmet of a hairdo jiggled. Finally, the world found peace when her fits of coughing eased up a little before completely halting only a second before the teenage kid in front laid down the first few notes of Canon in D.

What a cliché.

The crowd took the Canon in D as a cue to stand up, so I did as well. In all honesty, it was a welcome break from the lower-back-killing chair anyway. I let my eyes travel over the audience's heads and land on the couple at the very back, as in the bride…and the bride.

Zoe and Jemma.

The reason I attended this hellish event at all was because Zoe was one of my best friends, and she was one hell of a persuasive woman. We also worked together regularly as her company managed 83% of Ortega Records' artists. It just wasn't all fun and games when she used her persuasion skills *against* me and my best interests. The memory of her blackmailing me into this thing made me want to loosen my tie. It was still incredibly hot too, despite the fact that the sun was about to set into the ocean, painting the whole scene with long shadows and an orange glow.

They both looked gorgeous, I had to give them that. Zoe had clearly visited a hair salon since the last time I saw her, as the sides of her already short hair were cropped shorter and sharper than ever. Meanwhile Jemma's long deep purple hair was partially tied up in a bun that resembled a rose—don't ask me how that was possible—as the rest flowed freely and glimmered in the last rays of sunshine.

As I was admiring their outfits—a pair of complimenting tailored suits—the music suddenly morphed into something else right before the soon-to-be-married couple were about to walk down the aisle.

See, this was the part I'd been the most offended of in this particular wedding. The party absolutely swarmed with celebrities, at least half the guests musicians, many of them incredible singers—world famous vocalists—yet Zoe and Jemma chose some absolute nobody to sing at their wedding? All the while Zoe was almost exclusively working for *me*, managing most of our stars with her management company? So no one from *the* Ortega records, the sixth biggest record label in the entire United States of America, was good enough for their wedding? What a joke.

As I clapped out of duty, I searched the front to see who this Elle was that I'd heard so much about. The woman had earned an almost mythical reputation during the last few weeks when I'd questioned Zoe about their choice of ceremony musician. If she was truly as amazing of a singer as Zoe made her out to be, why wasn't she on Ortega Records' payroll already?

Given the praise I'd heard of this woman's singing, I wondered why she wasn't famous yet.

I mean, even if she was a little sore to look at, that would be very marketable. Which led me to think that maybe she was so utterly plain, so incredibly boring, that there was not a single point of interest to latch on to when selling music. Because Zoe most certainly knew she could introduce me to amazing talents in easier ways than making them sing at her godforsaken *wedding*.

However, the exquisitely gorgeous beauty, the platinum blond goddess with curves for days in all the right places who rose from the second row to head to the front, was anything but plain, let alone ugly. The tips of her curled hair almost grazed her waistline as they flew around in the brisk breeze. Her flowing, sparkly, deep ocean blue dress hugged her figure in such a way it evoked something primitive within me, an almost all-consuming urge to claim, to own, to pursue.

Then all my admiration towards the woman flushed down the drain once I recognized the song being sung from its first few notes. It was one of my late Mother's evergreens—*Whisper*. A powerful ballad that various artists had tried again and again to copy and rearrange, each cover failing harder than the last. Brave choice from Zoe and Jemma, which was the only reason why I even remotely tried to keep an open mind when the blonde beauty parted her bold-red painted lips to take a deep breath.

Well, in all honesty, I just hoped she was not about to ruin the entire song.

What I didn't anticipate was the absolute chokehold the woman had of my entire being from the first note forward. Truly, I did not pay attention to the couple walking down the aisle at all until they reached the wedding arch next to Elle.

She started soft, her voice vulnerable—fragile, even. As she built up to the chorus, her voice evolved with the song, until softening again for the second verse, only for her to almost cry out the boldest parts in the bridge before the last chorus. There were so many tones to decipher, and by the end a rich, deep, almost rough edge contrasted with the otherwise angelic voice. It stirred me from the inside, sending ripples of shivers down my spine, and reaching depths of my soul that I didn't even know existed in the first place. Even the tiniest hair stood up on my neck as I listened to the last notes of her song.

Yes, she truly made the song hers, and I did not want it to end in this lifetime.

I'd never encountered such a unique range of vocal tones from one single singer in my life—and as the heir to Ortega Records, I'd heard plenty during my 36 years of existence. She truly was the whole package, a rarity in the world of music. Though unpolished, like an uncut diamond, she was still stunning. There was nothing a few vocal lessons couldn't fix. She was, quite magnificently so, the first singer to take my breath away.

The corners of her eyes glimmered with emotion as she finished the song, and it dawned upon me:

Elle Wright.

I must sign her tonight.

HEIR'S PROPOSAL

My vocal cords were strained from all the talking I had to do. There were just *so* many curious people. The entire reception had been pure torture, designed specifically for me, yet I tried to smile through every conversation. I must admit, though, they felt like one interrogation after another. Utterly exhausting.

Funny how Jemma had conveniently failed to mention that the "few musicians" she'd said there would be in her wedding, actually meant a lot of A-listers from the City of Angels, *all* the higher ups from Ortega Records, and pretty much everyone from Zoe's management company.

My replies for them followed a similar pattern, each time becoming a little more painful than the last:

"Yeah, no, I'm not a singer."

"No, I'm not signed to any label."

"No, there's no album coming."

"I just like to sing, that's all."

I finally spotted a waitress doing rounds and saw a chance to escape.

With a curt nod and a brief "excuse me," I got rid of yet another leech and all but ran after the waitress. My champagne glass was empty anyway.

The waitress, a woman in her early twenties or so, reminded me a lot of myself back in the day when I used to do these sorts of odd jobs to get through college. She had mahogany hair though, instead of platinum blond locks, and was significantly thinner. She looked at me with pity in her eyes as I grabbed a glass and threw it back in one go, immediately grabbing another.

I knew what she thought of me. *"Poor little rich woman, having first world problems at an extravagant party. What does she even know about life?"*

Except I wasn't actually rich or anything. Even the dress was provided by Jemma, but the waitress didn't know that. I returned her pitying smile with a fraudulent smile of my own, before sneaking off through the side door and onto the lavish patio of the ridiculously luxurious mansion reserved entirely for Jemma's huge party.

There were some people hanging around by this over-the-top modern cube of a fireplace, but all I really wanted was some alone time. Thankfully, I managed to remain unnoticed while circling around the corner to an empty part of the patio. It was peaceful, and the light evening breeze made it easy to breathe after being inside for so long. I took a deep breath.

The night was beautiful, to say the least. In the distance, the ocean glimmered in the moonlight, but the city was sparklier with its bright lights. Vaguely, I heard the band start playing again after their break—yet another syrupy sweet love song.

Jemma totally owed me one. Or ten. I'd done well through the dinner and other formalities, but my nerves caught up with me as soon as I was alone. Even my hands shook a little, nearly causing me to waste some precious top-shelf champagne, so I laid my glass down on top of the thick white railing of the patio.

The grass on the other side of the railing looked incredibly neat. Very random, but I got the strongest urge to mess it up and make it less perfect. My heels clacked against the wooden floor of the patio. I kicked them off before indulging in my impulses, climbing over the railing to step on the grass.

It was cold and a little damp, but it somehow felt incredibly nice under my aching feet. It'd been so long since I'd last walked on grass barefooted. The bottom of my stomach fluttered in a warm way and my toes curled, the individual blades of grass tickling the spaces between.

"Amazing, isn't it?"

A *very* high-pitched screech escaped my lungs before I smacked my hand over my mouth in complete shock. I turned to look at the intruder—an incredibly handsome tanned man with dark features, maybe in his thirties. My eyes widened and heat crept up my neck from the ultimate embarrassment. I even vaguely recognized him; he'd been hanging with the Ortega Records crowd a lot.

The man looked down at me with his warm brown eyes twinkling in the dim lights of the patio. A smile played on his lips, too. He was clean shaven, but I could imagine him sporting a sexy stubble in his free time that did not include dressing up. His undoubtedly tailor-made suit perfectly accentuated his broad frame.

Yum.

Unlike me, he looked like he belonged in this kind of mansion and on this neatly kept grass with his neatly combed dark brown, very dark brown hair. I blinked and somehow managed to gather my scattered soul together before I gave in to the freakish urge to mess up his hair as I'd wanted to mess up the grass.

Then I finally realized that he'd asked me a question. "Um, what is?"

The stranger pointed down, a gesture which I automatically followed with my gaze. He, too, was barefooted. I looked around and noticed that his dress shoes were placed very carefully right next to my heels on the patio. The contrast between my casually discarded heels and his shiny expensive dress shoes set straight almost made me chuckle at the sight, but not quite.

"Yeah…" I said, trailing off.

That's when the band was done with the song and started another.

Holding out a hand, the man asked, "Can I have this dance?"

"Sure," I said, and took his hand.

It was warm. It was hard not to beam at him. He made smiling feel so goddamn easy. I could've danced with this type of man any day, anywhere. Even in the pristinely kept grass of a random LA mansion at my best friend's wedding.

The man led me further into the lawn and we began our slow dance, almost to the beat but not quite—it was hard to hear that far away. We only heard a little bit of bassline and some guitar, but the singing was drowned out by the other noises so much it was hard to make sense of the lyrics. Didn't matter much, though. We danced to our own rhythm well enough.

There was something very intimate in the way the man held my waist, but not in a creepy sexual harassment way. He was a little bit taller than me—quite a feat with my already 5'9" figure. He smelled like expensive cologne and new clothes.

I gravitated closer and closer, until I fully leaned against his broad, warm chest. One hand rested gently on his shoulder, and the other one fought so hard against this insane impulse to land on his chest. He had this natural pull on me, very hard to resist. Even if I knew very well he was way out of my league—plus a bit of an older gentleman. Not like old-old, but definitely in his late thirties. I also knew I shouldn't act so unguarded around super masculine alpha males oozing testosterone all the time, but I couldn't help but surrender to the moment.

I can deal with the consequences later.

"I believe you're the Elle everyone's talking about?" the man asked, breaking the magic around us a little, but not enough for me to be bothered.

Besides, his voice was only a low hum in my ears, very ticklish and enticing.

I fought off a shiver before replying. "I believe so, yes. Unfortunately."

"Not too keen on all the attention?"

Before I could stop it, a ringing giggle escaped me. Considering my hobby, and the way I'd lived my life to the fullest, I was far from modest. Some might even say that I was a bit of a drama queen and I had to admit that there was probably a bit of truth sprinkled in there somewhere. "Quite the contrary."

"Then what's the problem?" he asked, audibly confused. "Besides clearly outshining both of the brides, that is."

"Please, I'm hardly capable of outshining *Jemma,* of all people."

We both glanced inside through the huge windows and sure enough, spotted Jemma turning heads as she waltzed across the dance floor with her now wife, Zoe. Poor Zoe. She was in for a wild ride with the hurricane also known as my best friend, though I was sure she could handle it. I didn't know much about her, but I'd seen enough to be certain she'd be able to keep up with Jemma—and more importantly, keep her in check.

But the point still stood; even with my drama rich past, I didn't have to be worried about outshining Jemma, ever. Maybe that was why we got along so well.

"You do have a point there," the man said.

"I do." I nodded. "And the problem, you wanted to know, is that I didn't know I'd be singing for the entire music industry, that's all."

"You did great, though," he said.

When he smiled like that, only a little bit, there were a couple of fine lines in the corners of his eyes. Charming. "I did?"

The man leaned forward, looking directly at my soul. "The music industry is impressed."

The way he said it sounded like he *was* the entire music industry. I shook my head in slight amusement. He was cocky…so exactly my type of red flag.

"Enough about me," I said. "How about you tell me something about yourself?"

"Hmm… For starters, my name is Cameron Ortega," he said, and all I could think of was that maybe there was some truth in him actually being the entire music industry. "But people call me Cam."

"Hello Cam."

"Besides the name, what would you like to know?"

Preferably? Only his phone number, sexual orientation, kinks, and whether or not he was able to turn some of that cockiness of his into some hot bedroom fun. But as none of those questions were appropriate, I settled for a simpler, "What brings you here?"

"I'm a work acquaintance of the bride," Cam said. "Well, one of the brides. Zoe."

"Not to the wedding, silly," I said with the sweetest smile. "What brings you here, to dance barefoot on pristine grass with a girl you only know by name?"

"I would argue I know a lot more about you than a name now, considering the amount people have been talking about the mysterious singer today."

"Only rumors…and that's beside the point."

He spun us around a couple more times, bringing our dance to an end at the same time as the band finished their song. I still had no idea what this whole thing was about. Looking around, I realized we'd traveled across the entire huge lawn and had ended up beside the fence that separated the property from the cliffside. I tried not to feel disappointed at the loss of Cam's body heat against mine. The night had turned cold so I almost shivered when I leaned my elbows on top of the cold iron fence.

For a moment, we stared into the distance, to the moon and the dark glimmering waters of the ocean.

That was, until Cam spoke again. "I have a proposal for you."

I replied with, "And what could that possibly be?"

I had already started to mentally prepare for what was coming. The problem with passing as a cis-woman was exactly that—passing as a cis-woman. It meant constantly having to come out to random people, especially to the ones I wanted to date. I'd learned that the hard way.

So while I hoped that the vibes I'd felt meant that he was about to ask me on a date, I'd have to disclose being trans. It usually meant that one of two things was about to happen: 1. He'd be disgusted and take back his invite or 2. He was a chaser and would be more interested in whether or not I still had a dick intact or not than actually getting to know the real me.

Some people argued that there was a third option, which was that him asking me out was the start of some epic love story. It was an option where he wouldn't be phased by my identity in the slightest. Where it wouldn't bother him at all.

I'd lost hope for that option long before. My dating pool was very limited, and not only because I was trans, but also because of a…um…very *adult* hobby. It was hard being both trans *and* to have some special interests, okay.

However, what Cam proposed had nothing to do with dating me.

"Would you like me to make you a star?" he asked.

I blinked, rearranging my thoughts. "What do you mean?"

"I'd like to sign you as a recording artist for Ortega Records."

I took a step back, but Cam's eyes followed my every movement.

"You can't be serious," I said, my eyes widening in horror.

"Quite the contrary." He continued staring at me, face blank. "I'm very serious."

I first chuckled and then burst into a full blown, hysterical laughing fit. One that made me hold my stomach and fold in half as the corners of my eyes teared up.

"What's so funny?" Cam asked, still all serious.

I waved my hand dismissively, still laughing, and started tiptoeing back towards the patio. "Forget it."

"Slim chance," he said, following me. "I'm not going to let you walk out of this so easily."

At least he had the courtesy to help me back over the railing and onto the patio. I took his hand and climbed over, all awkward with my long dress. The humiliation of thinking he was about to ask me out was starting to settle in the pit of my stomach.

Once I was safely on the other side, I brushed my dress back in place and smiled at the man as sweetly as I could through my embarrassment.

"I'm not going to sign with you, Cam," I said, the absurdity of the whole thing making another laughing fit bubble inside me, which I suppressed.

He grabbed my elbow as I turned to leave. "I'll keep pestering you until you do."

I yanked my arm back and winked at the man. After all, it had been a while since a man had given me this much attention.

"You're welcome to try, but don't expect much."

MAIDEN'S REJECTION

Never in my life had I been as brutally rejected as I'd been last Saturday. Yet, I still couldn't get *her* out of my mind. I told myself, more than once, that it was solely because of her musical talent, and definitely not because of the way her skin burned my hands through the thin excuse for fabric her dress had been made of.

Surely it was only because of her singing voice, and not at all because of the adorable chiming little noise she made when she giggled. At the very least, it was *not* because of how heart-stoppingly stunning her green-blue eyes were as she looked up to meet my own.

I had no other choice.

Forgive me for I have sinned, Zoe and Jemma. I just have to disturb your honeymoon for a second.

Zoe looked rather reluctant as she opened the door for me and stopped me right at the threshold, pulling her black silk morning gown tighter around herself. Hair a mess, hardly wearing anything under that morning gown, she grunted at me.

"I don't even get a hello?" I asked. "You know it's afternoon already."

"Cam, it's our honeymoon," Zoe replied, greatly emphasizing the word *honeymoon*. "Don't you have even the slightest common courtesy to, like, fuck off?"

"I already gave you two full days, now give me Elle's number. And address. And her favorite color. Or, better yet, just tell me everything about her."

Zoe rubbed her temples and scrunched her eyebrows together. "Look, can't you like, contact her on social media or something and ask for the number all by yourself? Why do you need us?"

"She didn't accept any of my friend requests or reply to my DMs." Did I absolutely hate to admit this? Yes. But it was the ugly truth.

"So maybe she's hinting that you should fuck right off?" Zoe said, and the words hit my ego like no others. "Like I'm doing now. We were in the middle of something. Get the hint, please."

"No, never." I couldn't afford to think about my pride with this. Not when it came to Elle. There was no one else that could fill the void she left within me. "I need her. Besides, she's just playing hard to get. She basically said that herself."

"Cam..." Zoe whined.

"Look, she ran off like a goddamn CinderElle at midnight, so what else am I supposed to do now? Huh?" I was so frustrated I was about to start pulling my hair out. "Run around downtown LA asking all blond maidens whether or not the shoe fits?"

"Good idea!" Zoe said, and tried to slam the door in my face.

I was faster than her and put my foot in the way. I was not about to lose this chance, even if the sole of my foot felt like snapping in half. Not only was Elle the perfect addition to our cast of extremely talented artists, but I *bet* she was the answer to my prayers—the next star that would send *Papá* right into early retirement. The next star that would land the entirety of Ortega Records into my hands. *Papá* had been telling me that he wanted to retire, but he thought I still didn't have what it took. Pah.

Now if I could make Elle the brightest star of Ortega, I bet he'd finally realize that I definitely had what it took. I did. He only needed to see it. Elle was perfect for that task—equal parts risk and talent. But I was not afraid of a small risk; I was sure it would pay off.

"Please, let me talk with Jemma," I asked—no, pleaded.

I knew I had absolutely no chance in turning Zoe once she'd set her mind on something. But Jemma, on the other hand… She was known for being easily bribed. At least for the brief duration that I'd known her.

As if the stars aligned, it was Jemma herself who came to the door, wearing a similar satin morning gown as Zoe, but deep red.

"Cam! What are you doing here?" Jemma called out, throwing her long purple curls behind her shoulder.

"He wants Elle's contact information," Zoe said, and grabbed Jemma in her embrace from the side. "You're not going to give it to him. He's already ruined our honeymoon, let's not let him ruin Elle's week too."

"Oh, don't be such a mood killer, love," Jemma said, pretty much purring at Zoe's side, with a sticky sweet smile aimed at her. "Let's hear what the poor man has to say. I kind of want to hear this."

"See?" I asked, raising one of my eyebrows at Zoe. "Give me a chance."

"Then hit it, and hit it fast. You've got 10 seconds before I take my wife right back to bed and you can learn to survive without Elle."

I directed my best pleading face at Jemma.

"I just want to make your best friend the next brightest star of Ortega. Isn't it great? Every girl's dream." Except apparently Elle's but I wasn't about to let that stop me. "Can't you please give me her number, maybe an address, anything?"

"And what do I get in return for this highly valuable information?" Jemma asked, her mouth turning into a sneer.

"Look, I'm not leaving before I get some answers." I pushed past them, right into their hallway. "So either you're going to give that information to me, or this will turn into a polyamorous relationship real fast."

I saw Jemma's hand drop from Zoe's waist to her butt. "What do you say honey, how badly do we want to be left alone?"

The flame that ignited in Zoe's eyes was quite magnificent.

"Out, now," Zoe growled, and kicked me out. Literally.

"Ow!" I turned around to charge right back in, but Zoe was already about to pull the door closed. "This is assault!"

"And you're trespassing!" Zoe barked back.

"Vuitton bag and I'll text you!" Jemma hollered through the crack right before the door slammed in my face—and this time I wasn't fast enough to get in between.

But at that moment, the phone pinged in my pocket. Curiosity levels rising, I pulled the phone out of my jeans pocket and opened the message—a link to a purple and black handbag, which cost well over $2000. I almost got an entire heart attack.

However, it was a fair price if that could get me Elle.

I purchased it right then and there from the web shop and replied with the receipt. I didn't have to tap my foot against their porch before my phone pinged again with both an address and phone number.

I didn't hesitate for one second before hitting the call button—I didn't even bother to save the number first; it would be there in the call log anyway.

Within two rings, Elle answered with a simple, "Elle Wright," and I nearly entered heaven from hearing her voice again.

"Hello Elle," I all but purred.

"Who is this?" she asked.

Even hearing her annoyed voice sent butterflies to my stomach. "Are you ready to become famous yet?"

"Cam?"

"The one and only."

"Where did you get my number?"

"Louis Vuitton online-shop."

Elle sighed. "That fucking Jemma…"

I smiled at Elle's pissed off voice like a total nutcase. "Hey, let's not resort to profanities, shall we? You've got to take care of your image."

"No, I do not," Elle said, and let out an honest to God groan. "Because I'm not going to be famous, not now or ever."

"Yes, you are," I countered. "Name your price. Everyone's got one."

"Goodbye, Cam."

She hung up on me, but I still continued grinning as I walked back to my car. Elle had no idea how bad she'd messed with me at the wedding. She still didn't realize how far I was ready to take this thing to get her. She was, however, about to find out.

BESTIE'S APOLOGY

I was about to lose my mind sooner rather than later, due to the rate Cam was absolutely bombarding my phone, my social media accounts, my everything. He'd even bribed my goddamn doorman to bring me a draft of the contract he wanted me to sign yesterday. It went straight into the trash bin.

Look, I might've had a bit of a crush on him at the wedding, but it had all been flushed right down the drain once I'd learned he wanted me to become a singer for Ortega Records. It was a huge nope for me. Not only did I not want to become famous, not in the slightest, but I didn't even know how to make music…like, at all. I couldn't read notes, play any instrument, nothing.

If he was looking to get some, even on a friends-with-benefits basis, or had even suggested a one-night stand, I would've agreed in a heartbeat. Well, given he'd be okay with the fact that I still had a penis. But this, this was absurd, to say the least. There had to be some angle somewhere, because no sane person went this far to offer a *record deal* to an absolute stranger with zero skills.

Not that I didn't enjoy something about all this sudden attention, though. Still, this was some fairytale shit. I didn't live in a fairytale. I lived in an ugly and overly realistic adult world.

I snapped at the building's concierge José when the intercom rang. "Look, if it's Cam again, do not let him up. At any cost. Or I'm going to get you fired."

"Calm down Miss Wright," José said with his smooth customer service voice. "It's Mrs. Martinez."

"Who?" My eyebrows scrunched together for a second before I realized. "Oh, Jemma! I forgot she took Zoe's last name. Let her up, please. And I'm sorry for my outburst."

"No problem, Miss Wright. I'll send her up."

"Thank you."

But my mood was back to absolute crap once I lifted my finger up from the button of the intercom, because my phone started ringing. Again. With Cam's name flashing on the screen. I tried smashing the red button to end the call but he called again right away. So I let the fucker ring as long as it took for Jemma to come up.

When she did eventually reach my place and knocked on my door, the goddamn phone was still ringing in my hand. Nevertheless, I opened the door wide to let Jemma in. "I'll get the tea ready."

"Look, Elle," Jemma said. "I can't stay for long. I came to apologize."

Annoying. "How long do you have?"

"Like, 30 minutes."

"That's more than enough for tea," I said, and finally hit the green icon on my phone's screen. "Cam, Jemma is visiting. If you don't leave me alone for 30 minutes, I *will* file for a restraining order."

Jemma was laughing with her whole chest when I hung up on Cam without letting him have one word. I threw the phone on the side table.

"Do you have to be so harsh?" Jemma asked. "The poor man wants to 'make you a star' or whatever that cheesy line he used was."

"I don't want to be a fucking star. My life is finally comfortable," I said, and put the tea bags in our usual respective mugs—Jemma's had golden tits in all shapes and sizes drawn on a black base and mine had pink penises.

"Isn't being a world famous singer, like, literally every girl's childhood dream? How can you pass up this opportunity?"

"I know, it was mine too."

"Then what's the problem?!" Jemma exclaimed, throwing her arms up in her signature dramatic manner.

"Look, Jemma…" I handed the boobie-mug to her and we went to the couch. "My life is finally in order. I have a good, paying job and an awesome boss who will be on maternity leave for only a little while longer. I'm financially stable. I'm in a good place with the whole transitioning thing, and I finally pass as cis. I'm not ready to throw all that away for a slight chance at some silly childhood dream. I'm an adult now. I have to make adult choices."

Jemma's shoulders slumped. "But this is a once in a lifetime opportunity."

"Enough," I put my mug down on the coffee table. "Let's talk about this other issue instead."

Jemma grimaced—I bet she knew what was coming.

"Now, tell me," I said, and crossed my arms across my chest. "You seriously sold my contact information for pussy…and a *bag*?"

"Hey, it's my honeymoon," Jemma laughed. "Don't you think I get a free pass for wanting to get some?"

"But…*a bag.*"

"Hey, it was Louis, my favorite man. Vuitton. Don't insult the poor bag. It has done nothing to you."

"I hope it was expensive, at least, so Cam doesn't think I'm cheap."

"Oh, believe me, it was. I'm gonna suck him dry providing information about you," Jemma said with a chiming voice and chuckled. "I mean, I swear I'm not going to tell him anything else."

"I can't believe I regularly call you my best friend," I muttered, taking a sip from my cup. At least the tea tasted heavenly.

"Hey, isn't this what best friends are for?" Jemma asked. "I'm only thinking of your best interest. Like, aren't you tired of that boring corporate job of yours anyway? Live a little, hun. You used to be funny and interesting."

I gave Jemma a sharp glance. "And I'm not funny and interesting anymore? Thanks."

"Oh come on, you know what I mean. And don't tell me you aren't enjoying this."

"Well…" I started; she wasn't entirely wrong.

"Gotcha," she said, and leaned back. "Besides, Cam is hot, isn't he? I don't think I'm lesbian enough to not see that."

"Yeah, he is," I admitted. "But he doesn't want me that way."

"How can you know? Imagine all the time you'd get to hang with him if you worked for him? Maybe he'd find a different side of you."

"Doubt it. I gathered he's pretty high up in Ortega, considering it's literally his last name. He's probably not going to work with a total newbie. I bet after I've signed with him, he'll toss me at some intern or something and forget I ever existed."

"Nonsense, can't you see how much he obsesses over you?"

He did, there was no denying that. It had made me realize I had absolute crap taste in men, too. Because even if I was annoyed as hell at Cam's constant attempts at persuasion, I could not, for the life of me, forget how his hands felt like on my waist, how tasteful his cologne had smelled, the smoldering heat of his body against mine...

Yes, I definitely had shit taste in men.

And if I were to be completely honest, I didn't *hate* the banter, the attention...

My internal swooning faded as Lola decided to grace us with her furry yet adorable presence. The cat bumped her nose on my thigh, as if to say, *"It's okay."*

At least I still had her even if I was so painfully single that I'd pathetically latch on to every bit of masculine energy within calling distance.

LESBIAN'S BLESSING

I spun my office chair, leaving the cityscape behind me, to squint my eyes at the rude daydream intruder also called Zoe.

"Come on, there's plenty of fish in the sea, Cam," she said.

"Have you ever seen the news? The sea is full of microplastics and half the fish are on the brink of extinction."

Zoe leaned back in her chair on the other side of my desk and crossed her hands behind her neck. "Yes, but there's plenty of healthy creatures in LA. Just pick one and make them the main course."

I tapped the file I'd had my assistant compile on Elle. She was perfect down to her teeth. "But I have. To have. *Her.*"

"In your bed or as an Ortega Records artist?" Zoe smirked. "Due to this entire obsession, I'm not so certain anymore."

It was true I'd talked about her nonstop, trying my damn hardest to figure out a way to get her to sign, but I wouldn't say I was *obsessed*. Just enthusiastic to find the next star that would get *Papá* to retire and finally leave Ortega Records in my perfectly capable hands. In all honesty, I'd grown tired of him breathing down my neck at every turn.

Elle, though, was playing *very* hard to get. I'd dug up her email, bombarded her phone with endless calls and texts, but all my offers were turned down with a firm "thanks, but no thanks," in various forms. After she'd had her fun with me by giving me hope, she retreated in the end anyway.

Our latest text conversation was a good example:

Me: A holiday in Bali. Whole thing covered.
Elle: Throw in a long weekend in Paris and we'll talk.
Me: Deal. Now about the contract I sent you…
Elle: What happened to "hello, how are you?" At least take me to dinner first ;)
Me: If that's what it takes.
Elle: Still no deal. Bye, Cam.

I had tried every tactic, every strategy.

Luring her with money didn't work because she was way too comfortable in her current job. She didn't seem to want fame—which sort of was one of the reasons I wanted her even more. Extensive health insurance, lunches covered, free gym membership, whatever plastic surgery she could possibly desire, even the management paid for at her desired management company—I would've totally recommended Zoe's though—but Elle didn't want any of it. None.

I even stooped so low that I tried to dig up some dirt on her social media or something for some rather innocent persuasion purposes, but she had the cleanest internet presence in the history of the internet. There'd been a lot of cat memes. It was altogether useless.

"Look, whatever it takes, we're going to get her," I said, and crossed my arms over my chest. "You can think whatever you want about me or my methods. Just figure out a way and I'll *make sure* you will get paid handsomely as her management. Let's call this a mutual business interest."

There was a long silence, during which I stared at Zoe and she stared at me with equal intensity. I bet she already had something up her sleeve—she always did—and she only wanted to see how far I was willing to go to get Elle. She didn't seem to understand that there was no limit to how far I was willing to go to get Elle.

I *needed* Elle.

I guess Zoe found her answer in my eyes, since she broke eye contact first, picked up her phone, and started tapping. "There *is* this one thing, but I'll leave it up to you if you want to stoop *this* low."

She gave me her phone, and I clicked play on a video that looked like it was from her and Jemma's wedding ceremony. Probably filmed in secret; filming had been prohibited during the ceremony. The quality was very shaky and zoomed in enough to be grainy.

I thought I was ready. I truly did. I thought I remembered exactly how incredible Elle had sounded, but I was sorely mistaken. Even when filmed from the back row with a camera apparently made out of a potato, she sounded…celestial.

I was taken right back to that moment. It was like my guts had rearranged themselves back there, and I'd not been the same ever since. I was so thoroughly under her spell that I would've given my left arm to hear that voice live again.

Eventually, the video ended and I placed Zoe's phone in front of her on the desk slowly and carefully, as if the magic of Elle would break if I moved too fast.

"I can't believe you waited almost an entire week to show me this," I said.

"Sorry," Zoe said but she didn't sound sorry at all. In fact, I was fairly sure she was enjoying witnessing my ultimate suffering.

It didn't change the fact that she was absolutely right—what she was thinking would be stooping way too low even by our shady standards. "This is too much."

"Indeed," Zoe confirmed and pocketed her phone.

"I never even saw that if anyone asks," I continued.

"Translation: you want a copy of that video and I will send it to you." There was a twinkle in Zoe's eyes and everything. "It'll be our little secret."

She was certainly right, but there was no need to make her ego inflate any more than it already had. "Hmph."

"Anyway, I think you better warm her up some more beforehand. If we know anything about her substitute boss…" Zoe tapped on the file I had on Elle. "Having the video go viral could have serious consequences for Elle's career. Maybe visit her or something. Get involved in her life. Show her you're serious. Because, you know, this video might 'accidentally' end up on the internet and when it does, you'll have to be ready to take the fall."

A quiet grunt of agony left my throat. "I can't believe I'm having to go through such lengths just to get someone signed. Singers come to me."

"Think of it as dating or something," Zoe said, her voice dismissive. "You're good at that, aren't you."

Zoe had a point. Besides…Elle told me to take her to dinner, didn't she? Still, it was my turn to flash Zoe a small evil smile. "The same still stands; usually women come to me."

"True, though I've got no clue why." Zoe even scrunched her nose to drive the point home.

"It's the curse of lesbianism I bet." I fought off a smirk.

"The *blessing* of lesbianism. Speaking of which, I have to hurry home."

There was this dreamy haze on her face, and an unmistakable glow of love in her eyes at the thought of her wife. As I watched her walk to the door, I wondered if I'd ever look like that. Seemed very unhealthy.

"Oh, and don't forget," Zoe said, and turned on her heels at the threshold to my office. "We'll be off to the Bahamas next week. So please work your magic on Elle before that, alright? I'd like this settled so I can relax on our first vacation as a married couple."

Zoe left before I managed to mutter another word, but it didn't matter. If it was up to me, I was definitely going to get Elle sooner rather than later. A deadline would only help me.

Debonair's Invitation

Even I hated the sound my nails made when I drummed them against the desk in regular intervals. I couldn't help it. Even when Irene—my work bestfriend from the next cubicle—squinted at me with her eyebrows all scrunched together. It was the end of my lunch break on that very long Thursday and I'd received not one, single, lousy text from Cam. Not even an email. Nothing.

Was he seriously giving up already? Based on the pure number of times he'd tried to contact me this entire week, I'd thought he wasn't the type to give up so easily.

Damn Jemma. If she hadn't given the bastard Cam my number in the first place, I wouldn't have had to miss his calls either.

Not that I would actually mind him giving up this "let's make Elle the next star of Ortega Records" shit. It wasn't the singing that got me on edge with the whole thing, because I did like to sing. It wasn't even the publicity aspect that I had a problem with. After all, I was the public face of SCRN Inc anyway.

There were multiple other problems, however. First of all, I was not going back to the closet ever in this lifetime. Second of all, I doubted my very important, yet also very frowned upon, um, hobby…would work well with being an actual celebrity. I mean my workplace did know about it, but I was supposed to keep it sort of on the down low.

Also, there was the fact that I'd seriously thought Cam had been about to ask me out—I thought the chemistry was mutual—not for me to be his new shiny songbird. It was not often I'd felt so humiliated. Thank God I hadn't made my thirsting for him known. At least I didn't think I had.

"Miss Wright, come to my office. Now."

The tiny hairs on my neck stood right up upon hearing the annoyingly nasal voice of our new boss, Mr. Greg Montgomery. I rolled my eyes discreetly, well hidden within my cubicle, before hollering my hopefully not sarcastic sounding, "Yes, Sir."

I wondered what shit he had dug up on me this time as I stood up. I hoped I didn't look as annoyed as the knot in the bottom of my stomach suggested when I walked into his office. I missed Susan. Damn her husband for knocking her up and making me get stuck with this nuisance for the duration of her maternity leave.

My job as an in-house accountant for SCRN Inc, this big, modern and "innovative" marketing firm, wasn't anything fancy or particularly demanding apart from my publicity side gigs. Yet my mere existence seemed to rub Greg the wrongest way possible. He'd been constantly trying to find reasons to get me fired ever since he'd appeared to fill in for Susan.

Yes, I knew—everyone knew—that I landed this job not only because I was qualified, but also because I was publicly trans. That's right; I was the quota queer, so they could wave that pride flag during pride month to say they're "inclusive" without getting called out on their bullshit. Well, me and that one Navajo lesbian working in design one door down from the accounting department. Nina, I believe was her name. They loved to mention us in every article on SCRN Inc.

Greg never forgot to remind me of that fact. Or the fact that I was watched more closely than the others, due to the company image being dependent on me. This time, as usual, he did not disappoint.

"Nice pic," he said, and tapped the magazine he had open on his desk with his index finger once I walked in. "Or maybe you should forward the compliments to your plastic surgeon since there's about as much real in you as in a blow-up doll."

I couldn't help but glance at the picture out of curiosity. Looked like it was the one taken from the latest career fair for university students, where I was sent to flaunt the company's efforts in inclusivity. It *was* a great picture indeed, so I mustered up the sweetest smile I possibly could on the spot, and replied, "Thank you, I'll forward your compliments to Dr. Lewis upon my next appointment. Anything else?"

Even if disappointment over my indifference to his "burn" flashed on the asshole's face, I took it as victory. Sadly, he moved on to his next agenda all too quickly for my liking.

"This got delivered when you were on your lunch," Greg said, and pulled out a small black gift box with a pink satin bow on top. "I'll have to remind you that only business-related mail is allowed—company policy, you know. Please remind your, uh, partner, to keep private affairs just that: private."

"I—" I opened my mouth to remind Greg that I didn't have a partner, but in the end I decided I didn't want him to know how pathetically single I was. Instead, I extended my hand to get the box. "My apologies. May I?"

Greg pushed the black box across the desk. "Sure, just make sure it's the last time."

"I will," I said, and grabbed the box.

Thankfully, he waved at me dismissively right away and I couldn't have been happier to flee his den of an office as fast as I possibly could. I mean, I didn't exactly run, but I did walk very fast. I was also very curious to see what was inside the gift box, but one glance at the clock on the wall told me that my lunch hour was over, and I couldn't afford to get another scolding from Greg during the same day. My mental health wouldn't have survived.

There was only one problem, and it was the fact that the goddamn box seemed to grow in size every time I looked at it. I tossed it in my top drawer in hopes of it not distracting me as much. The effect of that, however, was that I was randomly very afraid of forgetting it, so I picked it back up and tossed it to the furthest and darkest corner of my desk. That was not a good place either, because I could still see it from the corner of my eye, but it would have to suffice.

"For fuck's sake Elle, open it so we can all focus on work," Irene hissed from behind my shoulder, effectively making me jump in my chair for at least an inch.

I leaned back and glanced in the direction of Greg's office. His door was closed, but you never knew.

As if reading my mind, Irene semi-whispered with a hissing tone, "I'll keep an eye on him, now open the goddamn box."

"Fine," I whispered back, and grabbed the box from the corner of my desk to plant it directly in front of me.

Now what? Suddenly I was all jittery. The satin ribbon was super smooth under my fingertips. Who even sent it?

Wait… What if this was some kind of prank? I leaned back a tiny amount to take another look at Greg's door. I swore internally that if there ended up being a spider or something inside the box, I was totally going to blame him. The jackass was out to get me on the slightest break of office rules. Which—during his reign at least—meant no excessive noises in the office. We were all to be as quiet as mice.

Irene lost her patience. "Elle, *now*. For fuck's sake."

"Alright!" I whisper-shouted. "Geez."

I pulled one end of the pink satin ribbon and the entire bow fell apart beautifully. I didn't know why, exactly, but my heart fluttered like a hummingbird's wings when I pulled up the lid. Inside, nestled in some tissue paper, was the tiniest silver microphone-shaped pendant attached to a long, thin silver chain—and a handwritten note:

I'll pick you up tomorrow at six p.m.
-Cam

BEAUTY'S OUTFIT

Zoe's idea of treating this Elle thing as dating wasn't necessarily the most brilliant idea ever. However, I had no better ideas left either. Therefore, I did find myself behind Elle's door with a pink rose in my hand. She'd finally cleared a free pass for me from the annoyingly non-bribable concierge of this building. It was exactly 5:58 in the evening and I was counting seconds until I'd see Elle again.

I told myself it was because I didn't want her to catch me being unpunctual.

Especially after the texts we'd exchanged earlier, the ones that got this undignified grin fixed on my face:

Elle: What happens at six on Friday?
Me: I see you received my gift.
Elle: Cut the bullshit.

Me: I want to show you something.
Elle: Like what?
Me: You'll see.
Elle: …
Me: It's a date.
Elle: I swear, if this is another way to get me to sign…
Me: You'll only find out if you come.
Elle: …
Me: Please?
Elle: What do I even wear?

I took that as a yes.

37 seconds before go time, I checked if my hair was still in place with my phone's self-facing camera. With 28 seconds to go, I wondered if all the pink was too much. After all, Jemma had said—only after the tiniest bit of bribing—that her favorite *color* was pink, not that her entire personality revolved around pink. Although it was altogether too late to ditch the rose anyway because there were only ten seconds left. I decided it was close enough to six p.m. and rang the doorbell.

"One second," Elle hollered, her voice muted coming through the door.

There was also a loud bang and some profanities before the door cracked open and I was met with a rather winded but still absolutely gorgeous Elle.

"Sorry, my cat's acting all crazy," she said, and yanked me by my arm. "Quick, come in or she's going to run away."

"Hi—" I said as I stumbled in, taking in the weird scenery of a terracotta pot cracked on the floor and all of its insides scattered on the vinyl floor while a white furry ball practically flew across the room like a lightning bolt.

Elle banged the door shut and leaned against it. "Hi."

I found the scene quite hilarious but didn't dare laugh. "Bad timing?"

"Nah, just everyday life in this household."

"In that case, here," I said, and handed the rose over. "More plants for your cat to destroy."

To that, Elle finally smiled. She looked absolutely stunning while smiling. The scary thought of wanting to see more of this smiley Elle took up about 87% of my brain capacity as I looked at her taking a deep sniff, almost burying her perfectly pointed button nose in the flower.

"Thank you," she said, as she walked into the kitchen corner of the living area of her very tiny apartment and started rummaging through the cupboard on the far right. "But I doubt it'll get destroyed, Lola prefers bigger messes. I bet she's not going to be interested in this tiny one."

"Good thing I didn't opt for the 50-rose bouquet, then," I said, and watched Elle fill up the tiny vase she'd found. By the time she was done, I had already taken in her cute outfit—a light gray top that hugged her figure, paired with tight, faded high rise jeans—and the beautiful little dip of her waist. Much to my ultimate surprise, she was also wearing the microphone pendant I'd given her, but I didn't dare to ogle that for too long because it hung right above a very enticing spot on her chest.

"Yeah," she said, and nodded towards the broken pot next to the couch. "Look, would you like to sit down for a minute while I clean up this mess? Or are we in a hurry?"

I ripped my eyes off her curves to glance at the clock above the tiny dining table and nodded. "Let me help you with the cleaning part, though. We'll be done quicker."

"Of course," she said, and handed me a black plastic bag. "Can you hold this open for me?"

"Sure thing."

I crouched down, right next to the disaster and Elle got to work with the broom, brushing the mess into a neat pile before starting to shovel it all into the bag. There was a short silence while we worked together to get the remains of the pot in one bag and the soil and the ruined green plant in another bag meant for compostable waste. That is, until I found Elle's actions slowed down quite a lot, enough for me to clearly notice she had something on her mind.

"What's wrong?" I asked.

"Nothing, I just—" Elle started but then completely froze for a second, her shoulders all hunched and head drooping. "I mean, if this is going to be an actual date and not like one of your schemes…"

One strand of blond hair had escaped her updo, so I brushed it behind her ear, hoping the gesture would somehow encourage her. "Go on, *mi princesa.*"

"There's something you should know…before…" she trailed off for a second. "I'm trans. I was born male, and I know that bothers some men—"

I pinched her jaw with my thumb and index finger to cut her off, then lifted her face enough to see her stunningly beautiful features. Her light blue, grayish green eyes first evaded me, but I didn't care. I cupped her cheek with my hand and brushed my thumb along her cheekbone, savoring the smoothness of her skin. "Did you really think I'd give two shits about that? Besides, I already know."

"You know…?" Her eyes narrowed. "Oh. Jemma."

I had a hard time not smiling at that. Jemma had, indeed, turned out very useful with all the intel she had to offer being Elle's best friend. The only thing I was mad at her for, was not introducing me to Elle ages ago. And Zoe too, for hiding such talent right under my nose. It was shameless coming from them.

"However," I started, not exactly uneasy but nervous of Elle's reaction. "To thank you for being so honest with me, I have to admit this will not be an actual date but yet another scheme."

I dropped my hand. She could do with that information what she wanted. In the end, after all was said and done, I wanted Elle to join our ranks at least somewhat voluntarily. It had to be her call in the end.

To my surprise though, Elle didn't seem phased at all, but rolled her pretty eyes at me. Adorable.

"Of course it's a scheme," she said, scooping up the rest of the mess into the plastic bag.

"I still think you're going to like what I've got planned, so please come." I stood up too and tied the bag.

Elle brushed her sweater straight. "Let's just say I don't have anything planned for today anyway, so…"

"So, shall we?" I asked.

"You never replied to what I should wear. Is this okay?"

I took another glance at her outfit as if I hadn't already eaten her out with my eyes earlier. What? I was not going to pass up the opportunity. "Very. Let's go."

I couldn't wait for her to see what I'd planned for our brilliant Friday evening.

VOLUNTEER'S LABOR

No cap, Cam managed to lure me into this shit purely by playing with my heart. First, it was him calling it a date—even when it very predictably turned out to be false advertising. Then the man took my breath away with a mere glance and caused heart palpitations with his slightest touch. My cheek he'd barely brushed so gently still burned, and we were already out of my apartment to whatever destination he had in mind.

There was one thing though, that I didn't quite understand, and that was the rather odd choice of a vehicle.

"What's with the van?" I asked, toying with my phone on the side, my goal to discreetly share my location with Jemma. It was probably wise even if I hadn't been occupying the front seat of a very suspicious black van whose contents I had not even seen. It didn't really help that the evening was fast approaching, either. "If you're about to off me in some dimly lit alleyway, just make sure they don't put a bra on my deceased-ass boobies for the funeral."

Cam's laughter momentarily filled up the space. "Don't worry, I'm not planning to murder you."

"Now, see, that's exactly what a murderer would say."

"Yes, but I still want to make you famous and for you to make me lots of money in return, remember?" Cam said, and winked, his smile lighting up his entire face in such a way that made the tiniest, most charming little lines appear at the corners of his eyes.

I turned to look through the window away from that one small wink that sent all kinds of critters to the pit of my stomach. No, not butterflies—critters. There was no freaking way I had fallen that deep with this silly little crush of mine. Especially when it did affirmatively seem like Cam only wanted me for my voice.

"Right."

Cam sighed. "The van is for all the booze."

My eyes instantly snapped back at Cam. "Booze?"

"And snacks. We're throwing a party."

"Party?" I was thoroughly baffled. I was also semi-sad because I knew I couldn't afford to get properly wasted with a whole session with Takaki-san planned for the next day. One I couldn't possibly skip because my mental health heavily relied on those sessions, especially when I had to deal with having Greg as a boss. A shame, truly.

"Yes. A party," Cam affirmed, then only briefly glanced at me with his still twinkling eyes before returning to look at the road. "I gathered from Jemma that you are somewhat familiar with Gina's music, is that correct?"

My heart skipped a beat. "Somewhat familiar?! I am the hugest fan."

Damn Jemma for spilling all my secrets. It was almost amazing how fast Cam managed to take my mind away from the party and dive it into something else entirely.

"Really?" Cam asked.

"Duh. Their voice is so unique, so rough. It's like Janis Joplin's, P!nk's and, like, Johnny Cash even, all put together but somehow better. Their technique is so new, so fresh and that makes their art so modern. Not to even mention the way they look, both masculine and feminine at the same time." I noticed Cam did that thing that men do when they've done something they're really proud of. The touching his chin with his hand while smirking -thing. "What?" I said.

"Oh, nothing. Please, continue," Cam said, quickly pulling his face back to zero. "I love to learn more about you."

Something smelled fishy. "Wait, what does Gina have to do with all this?"

Cam shrugged. "I'm passing the time here with chit-chat."

"There's more to it, isn't there?" I crossed my arms across my chest.

"Maybe," Cam said, but his look gave me the impression I was not getting anything more squeezed out of him.

I leaned back with a huff. "So I'm only here as free labor."

"Patience," Cam said with a small chuckle. "It'll be worth it, promise. We're almost there."

I had not paid any attention to our surroundings. "Almost where, exactly?"

"Here."

Cam pointed to the approaching gate that read "O.R. Properties LA" on a gold plate with black letters and pulled up by the intercom. He didn't talk with anyone, though, only picked up a card and flashed it on top of the number pad. The gate opened and we drove in, Cam nodding at the security guy sitting in his booth who barely glanced our way—it was obvious they were mutuals.

It looked like we'd entered some kind of gated community for filthy rich people. We were absolutely surrounded with gigantic lots with gigantic houses with gigantic garages and strategically planted gigantic palm trees. There was one house at the end of the road that was like the most ginormous out of them all, of which the driveway was absolutely swamped with cars and vans and black boxes with wheels under them. We headed there too, Cam maneuvering the van somewhat skillfully through all the mess and to a side entrance.

Once we hit full stop, Cam didn't wait for one second before he hopped out.

"Hurry up, we might get to see some of the filming if we act fast."

"Filming?" I asked while fumbling with the seatbelt, but Cam had already disappeared.

He did appear beside my door, just to open it for me, help me down and then he went directly to the back of the van. I followed him.

"I'll take the food containers. Can you handle the booze?" he asked.

"Sure." The huge styrofoam boxes which I suspected was the food, looked way too big and heavy for me anyway. I seriously needed to hit the gym sometime. "Where to, exactly?"

"I'll show you," Cam said, and took a couple of the smaller cardboard boxes.

It may have been a little pathetic, but I could only take one of the booze boxes when I followed Cam though the side door. It led to a storage room or a fancy big pantry. Further in and we ended up in a kitchen. An absolutely ginormous kitchen, with multiple ovens. Who needs multiple ovens?

Well, I guess *we* needed multiple ovens based on the number of black styrofoam heat boxes I'd seen in the back of the van. How huge of a party were we throwing again?

We didn't stop in the kitchen either. There were two doors in the kitchen, of which one was open and led into some kind of casual looking dining area, and the other one Cam opened. After a corridor with multiple more doors, one flight of stairs down and we finally stepped through the third on the left and into…a legit bar? I honestly would've thought I'd walked into a nightclub if I hadn't known better.

I shook my head at the sight. These rich people. If I'd lived there, I would've probably gotten lost and died of dehydration in some forgotten closet from which I couldn't find my way out.

Cam set his boxes on top of the bar. "Here. I'll get someone to help carry the boxes, but if you could start unpacking them that would be great. I'm going to handle the food and come help you in a sec."

I watched him go with slight wonder. I hadn't really figured out what was actually going on and what we were even doing here, except throwing a party. But for how many people, for how long, and what was my role in this? Above all, how the heck was this supposed to help Cam in his impossible quest to get me to sign with him?

Hilariously enough, I'd only felt like I was free labor, so far. But, I was already there so I figured I might as well start unpacking shit. So that's what I did.

TEMPTRESS'S JUDGMENT

Once I got the food in the ovens, I skipped the last few stairs in my weird eagerness to get back to Elle. I even landed with a bit of a thud, yet still, the two of them didn't even notice me entering the room—Elle engrossed in building a tower out of the champagne glasses, and Deacon leisurely about to sit on one of the stools by the counter, his disheveled hair looking like he'd only recently gotten out of bed. The hair-thing was probably at least half the truth. I guess I'd taken longer than I thought with the food upstairs because everything seemed to be set already and the two looked like they were just killing time.

"I'm Deacon, by the way. I help around the house. Mostly the yard and the pool. I take it you're Cam's new girl?" Deacon said, offering his hand over the bar for a handshake.

It piqued my interest to see what Elle's answer would be, so I refrained from making another sound.

"Elle," she said, and took his hand. "And I'm not Cam's new anything."

That prompted a short but noticeable twinkle to appear in Deacon's eyes and he pulled Elle's hand closer to him and lifted it up as if he was about to kiss it—the little rascal. "Really? But I thought he specifically said that Elle was about to be the next big star of Ortega."

Elle smiled sweetly at Deacon. "We'll see about the star thing, but even if I was, that doesn't make me Cam's girl."

I was annoyed at how good they looked together—and even more annoyed that I noticed such things. Deacon was way more age appropriate for Elle anyway—she was 24, as was Deacon—why did I have to care?

The smirk on my helper's face was evident when he leaned closer, his lips getting dangerously near to the flawless skin on Elle's slender hand. "In that case…"

The blood boiled in my veins. However good they looked together or how much more appropriate they would be, their time was up: I'd definitely let my pool boy play with my things for long enough. I cleared my throat which made both of them snap all the way apart from each other. Excellent. "Dee, could you check the food and bring it down here when it's all heated up in about thirty minutes?"

Deacon scrunched up his nose. "But it hardly needs anyone to stare at the oven for thirty minutes—"

I also tossed him the keys which he easily caught mid-air. "And park the van properly for me, will you?"

"Yes, sir," he said with a cheerful voice, but his shoulders gave away that he was slightly disappointed at the turn of events. "Nice to meet you Elle."

"Nice to meet you too," Elle said at his already receding back and started to polish another glass I guessed was about to go on the tower.

I sat across her in Deacon's previous spot. "You look like you've done this before."

"That's because I have," she said, and laid the glass on top of the pyramid. "In college, I used to do some bartending at events."

"Really? I guess I picked up the right girl for the job then."

"Nah, I'm not actually very good at this, it's just a couple of tricks here and there. I did a lot of odd jobs in college. Transitioning isn't cheap, you know. Bartending got me the best tips." She smiled, as if lost in the nostalgia of her time in college. I wanted to see her smile like that every day, preferably for memories we'd made together. That's how lost I was already.

I shook my head briefly. That was not the train of thought I'd expected, and I needed to stop that from progressing in any worse direction as soon as possible. Besides, Elle looked like she was done with the champagne tower anyway.

"Should we grab a couple of champagne bottles and some glasses upstairs?"

Elle put down the dish rag and leaned against her hands set on the bartop, to get closer to my face and squint. "Look, what's with all the mystery?"

Ah, time to play dumb. "What mystery?"

"First of all, what's going on upstairs and who are we even throwing this party for?" Elle said, grabbing a couple of coolers with champagne bottles already in them.

I moved a few glasses on to a tray. "I promised you we would get to see some filming, didn't I?"

"Filming what?" Elle said, scrunching her eyebrows. "A movie? Not porn, right?"

The mention of porn had me howling with laughter.

"No, not porn," I eventually managed to say, wiping a tear that'd escaped the corner of my eye. "That, I promise you."

Elle's eyebrows drew together. "A shame, really. This place looked perfect for porn from the outside."

My house looked like it was perfect to shoot porn in? I had a hard time containing another laughing fit. "Really?"

"What even is this place?" she asked.

"Apparently, a porn cave." I snickered.

Elle slapped my shoulder lightly. "Be serious for once, will you?"

Her expression was way too funny for me to reveal everything yet. Instead, I filled up the rest of the tray with glasses and stood up. "I am serious. And we need to go if we want to be there in time."

"Fine," she said with a bit of a whiny voice, circling the counter and dropping the two cooler buckets in my hands. "You take these, I take the glasses."

With my entire body still shaking a little from my earlier burst of laughter, I said, "Yeah, that's probably for the best. We need to be quiet when we go upstairs so we don't disturb the filming."

"Figured. Where to?" Elle asked, perfectly balancing the entire tray of champagne glasses in one hand.

I balanced both of the buckets in my left hand, leaning to my side, so I had one of my hands free to open the door. But before I opened it, I glanced over my shoulder at Elle. "And this porn cave? It's my home."

"Wait what—?" Elle asked, her voice all loud and high pitched, but I shushed her by planting my index finger across her juicy, smooth, and plump lips.

"Shh, we need to be quiet, remember?"

I took the profuse eye roll as a yes and slowly removed my finger before heading upstairs, swallowing the all-consuming urge to murmur "good girl" into her ear for keeping quiet so obediently. It amazed me how much Elle brought up some kind of almost primal itch to reach out to her…from somewhere very deep within me. The urge was getting harder and harder to suppress, but I didn't want to come onto her too strong. Part of it was because I didn't want to be seen as a total scumbag apart from my little need to get her to sign—*Mamá* had definitely raised me to be better than that—and I truly wanted her to work for me.

I kept telling myself all these urges were there, bothering me daily, only because of her voice. But the more I spent time with her, the more I texted with her, the more I talked with her on the phone… I realized more and more that there was something else to it. Something I couldn't put into words. Interest, maybe? Amusement? Certainly, I'd never met a woman quite like her before.

One thing was for sure though, and it was that once we reached the filming site upstairs and I got to witness Elle's eyes start to sparkle at the sight in front of her—I liked the glowy, warm feeling that settled in the pit of my stomach upon seeing that.

I liked it a lot. I liked it a scary lot.

INDIVIDUAL'S POETRY

My eyes widened and my heart exploded once I realized what was going on. It was something incredibly real, and madly thrilling. The sun was already low, just about to touch the horizon behind the huge infinity pool. The pool's water was still, reflecting the bright blue of the sky. There was also a captivating song playing, the vocalist's voice very familiar. It started off in English but later another voice joined in a foreign but beautiful language.

There were also countless members of the camera crew and huge loads of filming equipment. A drone hovered behind the pool in the air, the buzzing sound almost buried under the blasting music. An Asian person with long faded pink hair, knelt in front of a very handsome black-haired individual. They were two of the most gorgeous human beings I'd ever seen in my life.

That dark-haired individual, however, was the very same person whose lyrics and voice had saved me from the pits of my darkest days. An individual who was as handsome as the hottest men and as gorgeous as the finest women one can find on planet earth…without being either.

An individual who was otherwise known as Gina.

The language changed back to English, both of their voices in perfect harmony, and started building up to the chorus:

Even if the sky collapses
Stay for a little while more
Even if the earth crumbles
Hold me on the last edge
Join me, this is Trust Fall

Gina grabbed the white collar of the beautiful pink haired man, and both of them lip-synced to the lyrics as the man rose to stand tall, so tall their gazes met, before leaning back with arms extended to his sides. Once the high note hit by the end of the chorus, the man closed his eyes and Gina let go of the collar. The man fell back first at the pool, the drone following his figure down, most likely to catch whatever happened underwater from the outside as the pool had a glass wall.

Hmm…

I let my head tilt to the side as it felt like something was missing from the scene, but I couldn't quite put into words what it was.

At the same time, the middle-aged man sitting to our left, who I presumed was the director, yelled "Cut!" through the megaphone before turning to face the man on his right. "I don't know, something's not quite right."

Ha, I wasn't the only one who thought so.

"Yeah," the man next to him sighed, and leaned back in his chair.

He was absolutely chiseled. A gorgeous pile of muscles. The forest green tank top he was wearing, only accentuated his thick arms. Show off. His short brown hair was styled somewhat messily and black aviator sunglasses hung low on his nose as he looked over them towards the pool.

He didn't seem very concentrated on whatever the director was babbling at him, so I followed his line of sight.

I believe it was the pink haired beautiful man he was watching, intensely. I couldn't really blame him; the pink haired one was quite the sight with the white oversized button up having turned see-through upon getting wet, and clinging heavily to his lean figure. I glanced back at the brown haired one and had to fight a smile from stretching my lips as I saw him shift in his chair and hide his crotch with the tablet he was holding.

I knew that feeling all too well.

"We need another shot," the director informed the crew once he realized the Asian man beside him wasn't really responding. "Quick, before the sunset's over, please, everyone."

That started a whole entire war on the side, with two people pretty much tearing the wet clothes off the pink haired man's back, as another pair started blow drying his hair with actual four hair dryers at the same time while another person started patting his face dry and fixing his makeup, while yet two more people prepared an identical yet dry set of clothes from the clothes rack, ready to be jumped straight into.

"Joonie, fighting!" the brown-haired man next to the director yelled at the pink-haired one, earning a quick glance with sparkling eyes and a flash of ear-to-ear smile from the latter. Somehow, miraculously, it looked like both of them were enjoying this chaos. Which was good, because I suspected they were going through this all over again.

I was right. They did the whole entire scene and then the circus of changing clothes, blow drying hair and fixing makeup thing two more times, everyone growing more anxious every passing second that the director was not happy with how it turned out. Meanwhile the sun got lower and lower on the horizon. Eventually it was already like one third under, and I could taste the collective anxiety of everyone that sizzled in the air.

When the one apparently named Joonie climbed up from the pool for the third time, the director still didn't look all that content with the outcome. Even Gina was starting to pace back and forth beside the pool, looking deep in thought. Then it hit me—I grabbed Cam's arm instinctively and muttered, "They should both fall."

"What?"

"The lyrics say 'join me,' so shouldn't they both fall?"

Cam did this sort of slow blink as he processed what I was saying, and then his eyes started to sparkle.

"You're right," he said, and turned to the others before snapping his fingers twice and yelling, "Hey!"

At once, I regretted ever opening my goddamn mouth as every single pair of eyes at once turned at us.

"Elle here has an idea, does anyone care to hear it?" Cam said, and turned to look at me again. "I personally think it's brilliant."

The director took off his sunglasses and narrowed his eyes. "Okay, then, let's hear it. I think at this point we could use a new viewpoint anyway."

I swallowed the heavy lump that formed in my throat before speaking. "I mean, it says 'join me,' so I thought that maybe, um, could it be better if they'd fall together?"

There was a second of complete and total silence—sans the buzzing of the drone—before Gina clapped their hands together. "Genius!"

I would ordinarily have had a heart attack upon having a direct conversation with Gina, if it wasn't for the fact that their statement started a whole shouting debate between the entire crew and that took all my attention.

"But we don't have any spares for your outfit!" A stylist shouted.

The one who'd been patting Joonie's face dry between every shot was enthusiastically nodding beside her. "And we don't have time to do your makeup over and over again anymore."

"Not with the actual sunset but we can still continue filming with lights," the director said, and looked at his wristwatch. "However, I'd like to get this thing wrapped for today."

"You can use this house another day as well; it doesn't have to be wrapped today," Cam said.

"We have other schedules with Joonie before returning to Korea," the boner guy who'd been sitting beside the director said.

Eventually everyone turned to look at the director who had been staying incredibly quiet throughout the entire debate.

"We only have time for maybe one more shot anyway, so I suggest we go with Elle's idea. We do have good takes from the original anyway. We can just use them if this doesn't work out."

I guess the last call was the director's since after that everyone wordlessly followed through, preparing for the last take of the day. If I'd understood correctly, it was quite possibly the last take for the entire music video.

Once the slate board clapped, I got to witness the most magical scene unfold in front of my very own eyes, almost holding my breath. It started very similarly, Joonie on his knees in front of Gina, until they grabbed his collar and he rose, only to be held on the edge. Yet, this time, with the last bit of lyrics going "Join me, this is Trust Fall," Gina abruptly yanked Joonie against their chest and they both fell under.

When both Joonie's and Gina's heads popped up on the other end of the pool and the ripples set, the director pulled out his megaphone again and told us…
"That's a wrap."
I could finally breathe again.

Bartender's Retirement

At the after party, Elle fell naturally into the bartender role. I did not intend it. In fact, I would've told her to enjoy the party as a guest and made her stop, if only she didn't look like she was enjoying herself to the fullest. She beamed at the guests, made small talk with everyone, and mind you, used up all my fancy expensive booze to do these crazy gorgeous and interesting cocktails, each one fitting the recipients' general vibes to the teeth.

Like Joonie, one of the main stars of today—a member of the Korean group GRiD I'd persuaded (and poured a lot of money into) to make collabs with Ortega artists—received a margarita that was somehow glowing neon pink instead of the milky yellow it usually was. I guess Elle and Joonie had that much in common—the love for the color pink.

I'd planned on letting Elle mingle with the people today, who I knew were all very successful in this industry, but also purely good people. I'd hoped they could convince her to join Ortega Records too. I'd planned on taking a bit of distance after the music video shooting wrapped to make that happen without the pressure of my presence. But I somehow naturally gravitated towards her at every occasion with half-assed excuses. It made executing my grand plan somewhat strenuous, as I had to constantly remind myself it existed in the first place.

"She really saved today, don't you think?" A familiar voice asked.

I twitched in surprise. I had not noticed Gina appearing beside me.

"That's for your team and the director to decide, really," I said. "But in my honest opinion, Elle's idea was great."

"Is that why you can't take your eyes off her?" Gina said.

Their eyes sparkled a little too brightly for my liking so I avoided their direct gaze and cleared my throat before speaking. "I'm also trying to figure out a way to get her to sign with us."

"Is she any good, or are you just in love?"

"Oh, she's really good," I said, and pulled Gina through the door to the corridor before they could question the other thing too loudly. "Want to see?"

"Sure," Gina said, crossing their arms over their chest as they waited for me to shut the door behind us. "Though, what's with the secrecy?"

"She doesn't know I have this," I said, and pulled out my phone. "Here."

Gina took my phone and pressed play on the video. It didn't take them much time at all to breathe out an awed, "Wow, she really is good."

"Told you. Now, want to help me to convince her? She's a huge fan of yours."

"She is?" Gina asked while handing back my phone, grinning. "Couldn't have guessed because she has not approached me at all today. Which is sad because she's hot and totally bangable."

Instead of grinding my teeth together like I wanted to, I said, "You're going to be working under the same label soon. Better not start something you'll regret."

"Oh, come on… Are you afraid of little competition?" Gina asked with their grin only growing wider as they grabbed my wrist and pulled me back into the bar.

My declaration that, "There's no competition because I'm not participating," got completely ignored as they pulled me towards the counter.

I sat beside Joonie—who was engrossed in a conversation with his bandmate—while Gina took the stool on my left. Elle didn't notice us at first, but once she did, the only thing I could spot on her that said she was a fan of Gina's, was the way her eyes widened for a very short fraction of a second before she composed herself.

She fell right back into her bartending mode. "What can I get for you two?"

"I see you've been handing out some very unique drinks," I said.

"Yeah, I could use one of those personalized ones as well," Gina said, and smiled all too sweetly. "I'm curious."

Elle returned their smile with matching enthusiasm. It was almost like she didn't even notice me. "Any preferences?"

"Make it strong, so I can tolerate my boss more easily," Gina said, and even winked.

Elle nodded and got to work. As she was fetching some bottles from the other end of the shelves behind her back, I leaned a little towards Gina. "Hey, you were supposed to help me sign her, not scare her off."

"Oh, relax. I do suspect she does have a sense of humor. Very unlike you."

"I do have a sense of humor!"

"Dad jokes and sprinkling Spanish into conversations doesn't count as a sense of humor, Cam."

"No, but the Spanish is hot," Elle said.

She was back and I was momentarily stunned. My Spanish was hot?

Gina, however, laughed. "I guess it can be if you're into that pretentious stuff. Are you?"

"It depends," she replied and grabbed a spoon, balanced it at the edge of the tall glass she was mixing a drink in and started pouring something black over the white base very slowly. "If the person is able to pull it off convincingly."

"How about French, then, *ma chérie?*" Gina asked, leaning forward in a rather flirty way, their eyes glinting under the dim bar lights as they stared at Elle as if she was something to eat.

The dull burn of envy settled in my chest at the way Elle's neck blushed at Gina's words.

"French seems to work too. But I suspect it's only because it's you," Elle replied, casting her eyes down.

"Oh yeah, Cam here said you're a fan. Is that true?" Gina asked.

The glance Elle gave me was rather stabby in nature. "Did he now?"

"Hey, I thought it was common knowledge," I said, having a bit of a hard time trying not to chuckle as I threw my arms up defensively. "I'm innocent."

Despite the fact I absolutely detested Gina flirting with Elle, maybe even more than weddings, this was sort of fun. At least, it was fun to watch Elle pretend to be a bartender and admittedly it was also a little fun to watch her getting flustered even if I wasn't the cause of it.

I guess I was off the hook, because Elle said nothing more until she was done with Gina's drink and handed it to her. It was this perfect fade from deep black on top to pure white on the bottom of the glass. No frills.

"Here," Elle said. "And to answer your question, yes. I might be a bit of a fan."

Gina smiled and took a sip. Then their eyes widened. "Oh. Rum, something creamy and…cocoa?"

"Mhmm. So is it edible?" Elle asked.

"Very much so," Gina replied.

"What about me?" I interrupted.

"Here," Elle said. She slammed a shot glass in front of me and honest to God, pulled a hot sauce I didn't even know had been stocked in my bar and only filled the bottom fourth of the tiny glass. "Very fitting for your fiery soul."

Both Gina and I burst at the seams and started laughing like there was no tomorrow. The pure audacity of that woman. I threw my "shot" back in one go, and eyes watering from the burn, said, "Thanks, appreciated."

Elle nodded and glanced at her wristwatch. "In any case, my shift has to end here. I have to get up early tomorrow."

"You do?" I asked, admittedly a little disappointed and also surprised. But if she needed to go I couldn't possibly keep her even if I sorely wanted to, so I continued right away with, "Let me take you home, then."

"I can call a cab. Enjoy your night. Looks like the party's only starting," Elle said to me before turning her attention at Gina. "It was nice meeting you, Gina."

"Likewise," Gina replied and raised their glass. "Now if you'd just sign with Cam, we'd definitely meet more often…"

Elle first pursed her lips but then chuckled. "We'll see."

"And I'll see you home," I said, and stood up. "What date ends with the lady calling a cab?"

"A bad one," Elle said, and I finally earned a smile of my own from her. "Let's go then."

"Sure," I said, and turned to seek Deacon from the crowd. He wasn't hard to spot—looked like he was having some fun on the dance floor with one of the stylists. "Dee, take over from Elle, will you?"

Gina grabbed my elbow as I turned to leave after Elle.

"A date?" they asked.

My chest exploded with pride. And even if our "date" with Elle was not actually a real date, I marveled at Gina's disappointment. Just to take it a bit further, I put my hand on their shoulder in a very condescendingly consoling way and whispered, "*Jaque mate.*"

GENTLEMAN'S GOODNIGHT

While watching the buildings and palm trees fly by through the car's window, I had so much on my mind that I didn't notice Cam at all until he waved a hand in front of my nose. "What?"

"I was trying to ask; did my scheme work?" he asked.

No lie, I had totally forgotten the night had been a scheme to get me to sign with him. And continuing that no lie policy, I had to admit I'd had a great time. "Honestly, I don't know."

"Well, you did help me with the party, and I think you saved the entire ending of the music video. So either way, I have to thank you for today."

"Likewise; thank you. I had a great time."

"Good to hear."

"By the way…" There was still something that bothered me. "Why were they filming a music video in your house?"

"They needed a glass pool with a great view, and I happened to have one."

Cam shrugged, looking annoyingly good driving with only one hand, and resting the other in the middle, dangerously close to my thigh. The insides of whatever sports car we were in on our way to my place were considerably tighter than the van's.

"Besides, it was only that one scene," he continued. "So not as big of a deal as you're making it out to be."

"No big deal?" I asked, not quite managing to keep the annoyance out of my voice. "This is Gina we're talking about."

Cam sort of scoffed. "You know, your fangirling for Gina sounds semi-absurd knowing the bigger stars by any possible measure were definitely the Koreans."

"Joonie and Tae?" My head tilted in wonder.

"Yeah, they're from this Korean group GRiD," Cam explained. "Very big right now. One of the very few groups that have managed to successfully do a comeback after the mandatory military service the Koreans go through."

"Oh yeah, now that you mentioned their group's name, I think I've heard a couple of songs."

They were very pop, yet sung about pretty heavy topics, based on the lyrics of the recent songs at least. I had absolutely no idea what they'd done before but based on Cam's words about military and shit, I guessed they'd been around for quite a while. Maybe I should've listened to a couple more songs from them.

"They seemed very chill for superstars," I noted.

"They are. Been through a lot, however," Cam said.

"Yeah, I talked with Joonie for a bit when I made him a drink and he warned me about the dangers in this industry."

Honestly, I was more surprised about the fact that he used solely he/him pronouns. No judgment, he'd just mentioned that he didn't care about gender roles and norms, so I'd thought… I wasn't sure what I'd thought. Anyway, it turned out he also couldn't have given two shits about labels, and therefore pronouns. Had to admire that attitude.

"Such as?" Cam asked when I'd fallen silent.

"You know, the usual." I counted with my fingers. "Stalkers, enemies, drugs… Some predatory heirs to record labels who are trying to scheme against you…" A smirk made its way on my lips. What? It was way too good of an opportunity to pass.

Luckily Cam had an actual sense of humor despite Gina's earlier words, and I even spotted him pursing his lips together which I suspected was supposed to hide the smile that was very much trying to break through. "That last one sounds very dangerous, better keep your distance."

"Oh, I'm trying my hardest."

I glanced outside and noticed we were almost at my place already. For once, I was not over the moon to get to Saturday and a session with Takaki-san. I could've spent more time at the party, too, but the main reason was definitely Cam. Time seemed to fly with him. Too bad he didn't seem to be interested in anything more than a business relationship.

"We're here," Cam said as he parked in front of my apartment building.

I nodded and watched him circle the car and everything to open the door for me like the gentleman he was pretending to be. I figured it was better to enjoy this fake date as long as it lasted and smiled sweetly when I climbed up from the incredibly low set car.

"I guess it's a goodnight, then," I muttered.

"Not quite yet, *mi princesa*," Cam said, putting my hand through his elbow. "A gentleman sees the lady all the way to the door after a date."

José—the concierge—was already waiting with the door open, so I didn't want to start arguing with Cam in front of him.

Or, at least, that's what I told myself, but I think I wanted the moment to last just a little while longer.

"Good evening, Miss Wright," José said, and nodded at Cam. "Mr. Ortega."

"Evening," Cam and I greeted in surprising harmony.

The lift was already down so Cam led us both inside.

"So, this thing you have planned for tomorrow morning…will it take the whole day?" Cam asked once we were on our way up.

"No, it's from ten to however long it takes, but I'm most likely dead tired after it."

"Oh," Cam said. "Too bad because I could've figured out something for tomorrow evening. It's Saturday so one of our artists must be having a gig somewhere. I could've gotten us some very good spots." He even winked.

The lift stopped, the doors opened and I stepped out into the corridor, dragging Cam with me towards my door. The faster I got rid of him the faster there'd be no temptations to cancel my session with Takaki-san. The annoyance over having plans the next day only grew by the second he was there. Which completely threw me off because every time I saw Takaki-san, it was usually the highlight of the week.

"No can do," I eventually replied, congratulating myself on resisting the urge.

I stopped at my door and freed my hand before turning to face Cam.

"It's a rehearsal of sorts." It's not like I hid my favorite hobby from people, but I didn't actively try to bring it up either. To put it bluntly, it was not something to discuss over small talk. "For a…um…performance. Kind of."

"Performance, you say?" Cam leaned closer, almost cornering me against my own door. "Can I come watch?"

The world stopped right at that second. "Definitely not," I started, but then actually thought it through. Because maybe that little hobby of mine would finally sever Cam's plans on making me his next singing mannequin. And maybe he could start to see me in a different light. In a light that would get me railed right into a mattress. "Well, actually…"

"Please say yes," Cam said, his tone almost pleading as he put a stray strand of hair behind my ear. "I want to spend more time with you."

My breath was shaky when I exhaled. "Okay, come, but remember you asked to be there."

"Good," Cam said, and took a step back. "Night, then, Elle."

Instantly, I missed his closeness. So much so I couldn't help but blurt out, "You know, a gentleman would also kiss the lady goodnight after a successful date."

The flash of surprise only lasted for a second on his face, before he cupped the side of my face. "Would they now?"

I could only nod. My main focus was on the heat his hand radiated on my skin. I wanted nothing more than to lean against it and close my eyes.

"And was it *that* successful of a date?"

"Yes," I breathed out, giving in to the temptation.

My eyes fluttered closed, and my heart was hammering at a speed that must've been at least 150 beats per minute. Even my head felt light, as I waited for Cam's decision.

It took him a long, agony-filled while, but eventually I did feel a tickle of breath on my lips followed by a ghost of lips barely touching mine. And then it was over. The hand on my cheek disappeared. The carpet muffled the footsteps, but I could sense Cam had walked away.

I stayed still on that spot for a good while, holding my own hand on my cheek to keep the warmth of Cam with me for a second longer.

ARTIST'S WIFE

The next morning would've been significantly less awkward if only I hadn't kissed Elle. It had completely messed up this entire thing. The dating thing… It was a mistake. How was I supposed to get her to work for me if I couldn't even keep my goddamn paws and lips off her? I had a feeling that everything was bound to become ten times more complicated.

Why the hell did I kiss her?
Why the *hell* did I kiss her?
Why the hell did I *kiss* her?!

Yet, no matter how much I chanted that, the taste of her still lingered, all too sweet. I wanted to bang my forehead on the steering wheel so hard I'd pass out, but alas, that was not an option. Not if I didn't want to crash my beloved Bentley. We were driving so slow on this godforsaken old asphalt, that we wouldn't have died. Probably.

And what the hell was this "performance rehearsal" of Elle's about, if we were heading deeper and deeper into what looked like an old, somewhat abandoned industrial area. I could've thought of a thousand better places for rehearsing just about whatever, than this terrifying brick jungle in a heartbeat.

Yet, the navigation said that we were still heading to the address Elle had given me. She hadn't said anything about us taking a wrong turn either, so I continued the agonizingly slow motion forward. In fact, she hadn't said much of anything. She didn't look uncomfortable, though, only oddly impatient. She kept tapping her foot.

One circle around another pothole and a right turn later, Elle finally opened her all too juicy lips to speak.

"You can park right there, beside the door."

I wanted to ask, "what door?" because the way I saw it, there were no doors, just brick as far as the eye could see and huge windows made of teeny-tiny squares. Eventually, I spotted one. The door in question seemed to disappear into the brick as it was exactly the same shade though wooden, hidden in the corner of yet another huge brick hall. Above it, hung a small sign from rusty, screechy iron holders. It only contained three of those Chinese or Japanese or whatever characters carved into the wood and painted black, and a tiny western text reading "studio" below the characters written in simple capital letters.

"What is this place?" I asked, standing up from the Bentley and shading my eyes from the glaring West Coast sun with my hand.

"It's Takaki-san's studio. You'll see." Elle said, her voice rather cheerful as she skipped to the door. "You should consider yourself lucky to see one of my favorite places on planet earth."

Well, if this creepy place made Elle that happy, it couldn't be that bad now, could it? I took a wary step towards the door after locking my car, then a few more before the door shut behind Elle because apparently, she'd already made her way inside. Once I weaved through the crack between the surprisingly heavy door and the threshold, I looked around. The space I'd stepped into, appeared to be some kind of an entry room. It was definitely renovated but didn't stray too far from the overall industrial vibe.

"Leave your shoes here," Elle said, and yanked her own boots off as well, and stood by another door that presumably led further into this whatever creepy building. I only realized I'd frozen when Elle crossed her arms over her chest and raised one of her perfectly shaped eyebrows. "Hurry up, we don't have all day."

"Right," I muttered and proceeded to kick off my sneakers and place them on the low set shelf to our left, right next to Elle's.

She didn't wait a second longer than it took for me to get rid of my shoes, to open the door and waltz inside as if she owned the place. I followed suit. Let's face it, I was not going to run anywhere with my shoes off anyway.

However, the building wasn't even nearly as scary from the inside as it looked from the outside.

It was quite beautiful. The huge windows made of small squares, let in heaps of natural light inside the hall, casting a checkered pattern on the ash gray carpeted floor.

"Good morning, Takaki-san," Elle greeted and bowed slightly.

I too turned to look at the subject—a man, at least in his forties or maybe even fifties, setting up some kind of steel ring to hang by the ceiling at the end of a long heavy-duty chain, wearing only this thing that remotely looked like a full length deep blue bathrobe but of fancier material, paired with a wide black and gray belt that seemed to hold it together.

"Elle! You're here already," the mysterious Takaki-san said with a heavy Japanese accent, glancing down at us with a friendly smile on his face. "I'm finishing setting the—oh, you brought a friend, hello!"

"Hello, Takaki-san," I greeted, mimicking the way Elle said his name and bowed slightly, but probably looked way less gracious than her.

"Takaki-san, meet Mr. Cameron Ortega. Is it okay if he joins us today?"

"Of course it's okay, dear," Takaki-san said, and started climbing down from the ladder. "But I must say it's a first. Is he special?"

I swear I saw the older dude's eyes twinkle briefly. If I were to be completely honest, I had a hard time fighting a smile myself. Curious to see Elle's reaction, I turned to look at her, and was pleased to see her ears had turned red, much like last night.

Right before I'd kissed her.

No. That was not where my mind was supposed to go. Last night was the definition of dangerous territory right there. I turned my attention back to the older man who was still expecting an answer from Elle.

"Um…" Elle started. "Maybe?"

"I see," the man said, and offered his hand for a handshake. "Nice to meet you Cameron."

"Nice to meet you too."

His handshake was firm. I was surprised he even went for a handshake in the first place. Most Asians I'd met through work were all awkward if offered a handshake. Also, most Asians didn't use the first name right away.

I had to ask, "Have you been in the US for long?"

"Ah, for 12 years now," Takaki-san said, and let go of my arm to place both of his hands behind his back. He turned to look wistfully at the window. "In Japan, my kind of art is very underground. Here, I can make an honest living. It's not just at parties for that one specific group of people, but I get to do this for fashion shows, in movies, galleries…"

"Art?" I asked.

Instantly upon hearing my questioning tone, the man narrowed his eyes at Elle, piercing her only with his glare, so sharply she took a step back. "You didn't explain to him?"

Elle licked her bottom lip nervously. Adorable. I'd never seen her like that before.

"Um, I thought, maybe you could do it for me?" she asked, her voice so sweet I was about to get a toothache at any minute.

Takaki-san, however, was unfazed. "Elle, you know you shouldn't bring people into this blind. It's irresponsible, not to mention dangerous."

"I know." Now she looked so pitifully defeated and regretful that my heart experienced the pain with her.

"I'll let this slide this one time, Elle, since it's your first guest," Takaki-san said, and gave her a reassuring nod. "Now, go change—I brought a special gift for you all the way from Kyoto, I wish you could wear it for this session."

"Really? Nice," Elle said, and started walking towards a set of dividers that was set at the side, which I assumed was for changing clothes. But not many steps later, she stopped, and turned to look at the thing hanging from the ceiling beside the ladder. "The ring…does this mean I get to spin today?"

"If you behave better from now on," Takaki-san replied.

"Cool," she said, and skipped the rest of the way to the changing cubicle thing.

Takaki-san and I were left to watch after her in ultimate wonder—me wondering whatever this whole thing was that got

Elle so hyperactively cute, and the older man seemingly in awe of Elle's misbehaving.

Eventually, Takaki-san sighed and said, "A mischievous woman, that one is."

"She is," I confirmed.

"Shall we?" Takaki-san asked and gestured towards the other end of the hall towards a double door in the middle.

I nodded and we walked side by side, in silence. To say I was curious would've been an understatement. I had a feeling I was about to learn something totally new about Elle, something exciting.

"So, tell me Cameron-san, how much have you heard about kinbaku-bi?" Takaki-san asked once we reached the door and stopped to face me with a rather peculiar expression on his face.

I had to admit, that possibly Japanese word didn't ring any bells. "Huh?"

"Shibari?"

That one had a familiar sound to it, but I couldn't quite put my finger on it.

"BDSM?"

"Wait…"

"Bondage, discipline, dominance, submission, sadism, masochism."

My breath hitched to my throat. Was that what this was about? Was I about to step into some perverted dark dungeon? Was this the time when I was supposed to grab Elle and run away, screaming? "Um, I have watched porn, yes."

"What I do, what Elle does, has little to nothing to do with porn. However, I gather you are familiar enough with the topic at hand, then."

Takaki-san opened the doors wide open. Momentarily, I was blinded by the super strong lights that automatically turned on once we stepped inside.

"Welcome to my gallery," Takaki-san said.

My vision finally focused, and I was stunned, absolutely speechless. At a glance, it was an even bigger hall compared to the previous one, and all four walls were filled with photographs. What took most of my attention was the constellation in the middle, made of what must've been at least a hundred yards of deep red rope. At first it looked like the fancy giant 3D web of a spider, until when looking at it from the right angle, I noticed an empty shape in the center of the entire thing—the shape of a crescent moon.

"That is…quite something," I finally managed to choke out.

"Quite the centerpiece, isn't it?" Takaki-san asked.

"Definitely."

"This is my world of kinbaku-bi, the art of tight binding. Usually done with people as the subject, though. Such as our lovely model of today; Elle."

"So, bondage?"

"In my humble opinion, the most beautiful form of it," he confirmed. "What I mostly do is traditional Japanese rope bondage. Lately though, I've been experimenting with these kinds of abstract things on the side."

"It's beautiful."

Takaki-san sort of hmphed dismissively and started walking towards the wall on the left. "It keeps the boredom away."

I followed him. This wall was entirely filled with photographs of a woman, naked in most of the pictures and tied in various different…uh…poses. Or even hanging from some bamboo sticks or from a similar ring that was now set on the other hall. She had a huge tattoo on her back—quite the identifier since the photos seemed to date back what seemed like decades, with the woman aging a little towards the right end of the wall.

"That's a beautiful tattoo," I wondered aloud.

Takaki-san nodded. "A rarity."

I blinked and looked at the man who plainly continued staring at the pictures, his eyes warm with affection. "This is my late wife, Aikyo Ichika."

I blinked and looked away. Suddenly, I found my feet and the floor very interesting. I couldn't quite believe I'd stared at this old man's dead-ass wife's rope-tied tits in awe.

"It's okay, you can look." Takaki-san said, and chuckled after apparently reading my mind. "The pictures are hung up there for that exact reason."

I raised my eyes but couldn't quite look at the pictures with the same interest as before. While Ichika's pictures were gorgeous, I was glad to move on, so I wordlessly followed the older gentleman towards the next wall of photos.

"Now, this is Valeria," Takaki-san said, and moved on to the wall in the back of the hall.

This time, I was more careful and only briefly glanced at the pictures. This wall had significantly less, all of them starred by a rather voluptuous yet very gorgeous long-haired Latina. I stood by, waiting for more information before taking greater interest—Takaki-san seemed to like surprises. Me and surprises, however, we weren't the greatest friends.

"Valeria is my most recent model," Takaki-san explained. "I found her at this kink club. The poor thing was cast away by her former rigger because she gained some weight. Such a shame, I find her rather beautiful."

Okay, maybe this one was, indeed, safe to look at more closely. "She is, indeed, very beautiful."

Takaki-san nodded.

"So, what exactly is your relationship with Valeria?" I had to ask.

"Valeria, or someone else?" Takaki-san shot me with a side-eyed glance before continuing. "All my models are just that to me; models. Muses, if you will. There is nothing sexual or romantic going on between Elle and I, if that's what you're wondering. While this type of art can be erotic in nature, and we do share a certain type of connection, we are not in a romantic relationship in the traditional sense."

That was exactly what I was wondering.

"For some people, being bound is like meditation," Takaki-san explained further. "For some, it's a confidence boost. And for others, it is a way to find their true selves. Which brings us to Elle."

While not quite sure I was ready to see my hopefully future employee—and a woman whose lips tasted like cotton candy and dreams—naked, I still sheepishly followed Takaki-san to the wall on the far right. When in Rome, right?

Elle's wall was quite something. Filled from floor to ceiling, like Ichika's, for starters. But she was rather, um, clothed, compared to Ichika and Valeria. Which, don't get me wrong, was a relief for me but I couldn't stop wondering about that. Her genitalia was always hidden, and, well, breasts were on display only at the right side of the wall which I suspected were the most recent photos based on the fact that Ichika's wall had been arranged in chronological order.

Once again, I pulled my eyes away after only a glance—but there was no escaping the fact that the images had already imprinted on my retinas. I suspected they'd be there for a while. Goddammit.

"If not counting my wife, Elle has been with me the longest," Takaki-san said. "Since she was twenty, so for four years now. Most of them leave once they've found whatever they were after from me."

I only nodded, totally lost for words. I had a million possible questions, but somehow I couldn't get any of them turned into complete sentences. Plus, I was already quite jittery even thinking about the fact that I was about to witness this hardcore bondage thing happen to Elle. There was a huge lump forming at the back of my throat.

"I suspect that Elle is going to leave me soon, too," Takaki-san continued, his piercing stare directed straight at me.

RIGGER'S ROPES

Whatever the garment was that Takaki-san wanted me to wear, was in a black gift box with a pink bow on top. My hand automatically reached for the microphone pendant that had arrived in a similar though a much smaller box—I'd gotten a lot of gifts lately. The silver was cold under my fingertips, but I could only focus on the heat that my body was radiating behind the silver; it burned.

I guess I was more nervous than I'd originally anticipated.

Takaki-san was right; I'd never brought any guests to our one-on-one sessions, despite him saying it would be fine countless times before. Not even Jemma had been to any of these, and she was my best friend for life. So why on earth had I thought it would be totally fine to bring in Cam—who was essentially still a complete stranger?

It was not like I had never performed for a live audience with Takaki-san—quite the opposite. Somehow, it was still not the same. There was always a crowd at the performances we did, dimmed lights and like-minded people. Especially in the ones we did in kink clubs.

This was way more intimate.

Yet, I knew I couldn't back out anymore. I'd already dragged Cam into this mess that was my life; why not go through with it. And so far, I hadn't heard any screeching screams of deep shock from the gallery I'd heard them go in, which must've been a good sign. Right?

My hands only shook a little when I lifted the lid of the gift box. Underneath was a layer of smooth thin white paper, that let through only the tiniest bit of light pink from the item below. Getting slightly excited, I quickly got rid of the paper to get to the…silk?

Yes, it was definitely silk. The material was so smooth and velvety under my touch. Like, despite my lack of knowledge, I was pretty damn convinced it was actual pure silk with what looked like hand-painted cherry trees in full bloom. It was stunning.

It was not a kimono—that much I knew for sure. Enough fabric to make a kimono topped with this much detail would've cost an entire fortune. What it was, or looked like, was an incredibly fancy dressing gown. I kicked off my jeans and t-shirt so fast, just to feel the material on my skin. I shivered when I pulled it on. It was soft, smooth, but also a bit chilly against my body.

"Elle-san, we are ready when you are," Takaki-san said.

Shit. I guess I'd taken a lot more time admiring the garment than I should've. That, or Takaki-san and Cam had been fairly efficient with their tour in the gallery. Whether that was a good or a bad sign, I had absolutely no idea. "I'm almost ready!"

I closed the front of the gown, then tied the thin white silk rope that held it all together at the front in a very sloppy bow. Then made sure my downstairs stuff was still nicely, securely tucked. The necklace Cam gave me, I laid carefully on top of the black gift box, before I stepped out in the open from behind the dividers. Last minute, I even conjured a smile on my face, hoping it would mask my nervousness somehow.

"You didn't run away yet?" I asked Cam when I stepped directly under the steel ring, hopefully in a playful manner. At least my voice didn't shake.

Cam's lips turned into a sweet, sweet smile. "You've only made me more curious, *mi hermosa.*"

"I did?"

Cam didn't get to reply, before Takaki-san pulled us both back to the present from our own little world.

"Shall we?" he asked, picking up one of the hemp ropes he'd laid ready on the floor, before turning to Cam. "There's foldable chairs behind the dividers if you'd rather sit."

"I'll keep that in mind," Cam replied, still staring directly at me, and made no effort to move from his spot only a few feet from me and Takaki-san.

The heat rushed to my face. Yeah, I certainly hadn't thought this through, when thinking this would be similar to performing for a crowd. It was *so* not the same. There were literally only three of us, total, of which one was *Cam.* The subject of my daydreams -Cam.

"Private, or performance rules?" Takaki-san asked, sliding the bundle of rope against my back. It was his way of getting me used to the feeling of the rope. Our little ritual. It somehow grounded me, and the muscles on my back relaxed. Not by a lot, but enough for me to feel slightly less nervous. I was grateful.

And what he was referring to, was our two sets of rules; one set for public performances or photoshoots, and one set for our private sessions. Both lists were extensive, but the main point was that I wasn't very comfortable showing my genitalia in public—mostly because my workplace probably wouldn't have approved, but also because I was still not that comfortable with my downstairs area enough to show it off, even when I'd somehow learned to live with it.

Tits, however, were designer quality. I didn't pay close to ten grand—and had almost died to post-op complications—only to hide them. They were free for all, in all circumstances. If I could, I would've sauntered topless all the time.

"Performance rules." I replied.

I did not have to think for long about which set of rules I wanted to follow that day. If Cam wanted to see me completely naked, he'd have to warm up my bed for a few hours first. Preferably in a rather rough manner.

Another wave of heat flooded my face upon that thought. Thankfully, I didn't have to wallow in that particular self-induced misery for long, since all that evaporated from my mind once the skin on my collarbone first made contact with the rope Takaki-san laid there to wait for further use.

"Relax, and forget he's here," he whispered in my ear, probably loud enough for Cam to hear, because he was, in all actuality, right there…but quietly enough for it to soothe my nerves rather than make me more aware of Cam's presence.

I didn't have to be told twice. I was already heading to my happy place. With each knot Takaki-san made for the chest harness on top of the silk robe—a basic but reinforced shinju harness meant for suspension which I would've recognized in my dreams at this point, just by the feel of it—I fell more into that headspace, to that place where none of my worries, none of my insecurities, not even my happiness, mattered.

It was where my body took control from my mind. Where my instincts took over rational sense. Where I became too overwhelmed by the immobility, by the pain, by the physical strain Takaki-san so skillfully put me through, that I could not, for the life of me, give a fuck. About anything.

Only vaguely, I registered a thing here or there; maybe recognition of some of the ties Takaki-san was making, or when he asked if I was still doing okay. Or for my safeword, which I didn't use—it was a pretty basic suspension, nothing I hadn't handled before. I guessed it was more aimed to amuse Cam rather than for my enjoyment, and for that I was grateful. I hadn't brought Cam here for him to be mentally scarred for the rest of his life.

Otherwise, I was completely out of it. That was the beauty of this. The factor that had gotten me completely hooked from the moment I'd first been tied up by Takaki-san. Later on, I'd also found the more sensual aspect of this, but it was never fully about the eroticism—it was always more about the art, the free therapy, and the meditative aspect. For me, that is, at least with Takaki-san.

Sadly, it was over all too soon.

The drop from the high wasn't like a crash, but rather a slow descent that accelerated the fall a little more with each part of the tie he opened. About halfway through the untying process, I realized my chest had fallen out of the "outfit," if you could call the dressing gown and a gaff an outfit in the first place. Not long after, the fact that Cam was still there too, also registered in my brain.

However, the remainders of the restraint high made sure I was no longer bothered by Cam's presence in the slightest— and it was not like I could do shit about my tits hanging out anyway with them tightly tied still.

As a matter of fact, my brain was for once as clear as day in Cam's presence. I could actually think. More than I'd been able to ever before in his company. I realized a couple of things— that I'd be better off at least considering his offer of signing with Ortega Records, and that I might've been too harsh on him. My mind began mustering questions upon questions, until I couldn't keep it in.

"Takaki-san," I said—well, more like whined—when there was only the chest harness, the thick band on my waist and only one band on my leg still tied to the ring above. "Can't I spin here for a moment?"

"Are you sure you can handle it?"

"Yes." If I extended my already freed leg, I could reach the floor, even.

"Sure thing. I'll go make us some tea." Takaki-san turned to face Cam. "Care to join me?"

"Sure, though can she get down on her own?" Cam asked.

"Most certainly." Takaki-san assured Cam. "And we're not going far."

"No, Cam stays," I said, and leaned my body weight a little towards the left which made me spin the other direction very slowly. "I want to interrogate him."

"What? Can't you come down for it?" Cam asked. If I had even the slightest idea of how people's tone of voice worked, he sounded slightly panicked.

It made me want to smile, but I needed to be serious for this, so I pulled my face blank. "I prefer it this way."

"This is, um, rather distracting. So please don't hold me accountable for my replies. Can't you at least…like…cover your, er, upper body? A little bit? Maybe?"

"What, you can't handle my hand-crafted designer tiddies long enough to answer a few questions? I happen to believe I'll get more truthful answers this way."

"I don't know," he said, and scratched the back of his head. "You know, this can surely wait until—"

"Look, do you still want me to sign a deal with Ortega Records?"

"Yes."

"Then we'll do it this way." And that was final.

Cam sighed. "Fine. Suit yourself."

"I'll leave you two to it," Takaki-san said, and I was sure I saw his lips twitch a little before he bowed and backed away to the small kitchenette beside the entrance. He was clearly giving us privacy without completely abandoning me at Cam's mercy tied up—I bet the old fox found all this amusing. I couldn't really blame him.

Either way, I had more urgent matters to discuss with Cam.

"First question, and I can't believe I haven't asked this before: Why do you even want me to sign with Ortega Records?"

Cam was completely silent for a second or two, before asking, "Do you want fancy words or the brutal truth?"

"Both," I said.

"Fine, but remember you asked for it."

"Cam, stop stalling. Please."

"Okay, okay." Cam crossed his arms on his chest. "I really do believe you're talented, and your voice is very unique. On top of that, you're hot and clearly fit enough to pull off performances, long concerts, even tours."

Cam thought I was hot? "And the brutal truth?"

"You can also become my ticket to get rid of *Papá*."

"What do you mean?"

"Look, you're the perfect candidate to become a superstar. You're interesting, unique, talented and come with an intriguing backstory. The press will have fun with you for days on end. Ortega hasn't really gotten a proper superstar in the market since Gina, though we are doing fairly well with other artists too…it's just not quite like Gina. I figured, if I can pull this off, my father could finally retire for good and leave me alone."

It didn't surprise me that there were ulterior motives behind all this. But I was a little disappointed—disappointed in the same way I was when I realized he didn't want to take me on a date back at Jemma's wedding—but not disappointed enough to tell him to get lost for good. Also, he saw me as a potential equal to *Gina?!*

"Fair enough," I eventually muttered.

"Any other questions?"

"How does one even become a singer, let alone a star?" I asked. "Like, I have never even played one instrument. I have no idea how to compose songs. I have never even written one poem since the mandatory high school ones. Besides, I'm hardly any teenage dream material with my trans-ass and this very adult hobby."

"Many artists these days don't compose their own music, and Ortega works with the best songwriters in the industry— so that will be covered. However, you are welcome and will have the resources to learn to do music and learn instruments if you want. We can always at least alter the lyrics to make them more you."

"Sure…" I was not sure in the slightest.

"We already have Gina so I bet you being trans won't be too big of a problem. Surely you know it'll take some opportunities away from us, but I'd say not many these days."

"Right."

"And regarding your adult hobby… I was not thinking of targeting teens with your music anyway. I bet we could even use this to our advantage, somehow. Sex still sells. Anything else?"

"I—not now, I guess." I stopped myself from spinning by letting my toes land on the carpeted floor. I was drawing a total blank, so suddenly, despite having tons of questions in my head earlier. I guess I hadn't really anticipated that Cam had actually thought these things through already.

"So, does this mean you'll finally sign with me?"

"No!" I said, and heaved myself more upwards by the ropes, so I could reach for the band on my thigh. "It means I will consider it."

"That was all I ever asked in the first place."

"Good," I said, pulled from a certain knot and the tie on my leg all but unraveled by itself. Rope was so easy to get out of when you knew what you were doing…that is, if the rigger left ways to escape.

I couldn't say the same about Cam. That man was doing his damn hardest to leave no exits whatsoever. The worst part was that I was no longer sure at all if I even wanted to get out.

FOOL'S IDEA

Elle kept rubbing her arms in between sipping tea when she sat across from me in the trendy café by her apartment complex. I'd taken her there after the whole thing at Takaki-san's studio, because after everything I'd been through there, she totally owed me this. Some normalcy. Not that I complained about our earlier activities either. I'd learned a lot about her, which was, of course, nice…but admittedly being interrogated with the most perfect pair of tits directly at my eye level had been an experiment and a half.

She focused mostly on the spot above her wrists and another spot above her elbows. It was somewhat distracting, as the faded red marks left there painted my imagination with the scene I'd witnessed earlier that day, in vivid detail. Even if no one could've possibly noticed or even figured out what caused them, I saw them as clear as day. I could still picture the ropes snaking on her body in enticing patterns, easily. I admit I'd been skeptical at first, when Takaki-san called the whole thing with the ropes art, but afterwards I totally understood what he meant.

It *was* art. Erotic, enchanting, and enticing art, but art nevertheless.

"How long do the marks stay?" I asked, taking a sip of my scalding hot espresso. I needed a distraction and maybe focusing on the downsides of said art would give me some.

"It depends," Elle said, and brushed the marks above her wrist, smiling. "For a simple suspension like that, usually less than a day. They're already quite faded, don't you think?"

I very nearly coughed up the half cup of espresso I'd consumed so far, but somehow miraculously managed not to. That had been simple?! "Right."

"I like them. The patterns the ropes leave. Sadly they only last a little while."

To me, they just looked painful. "Why, though?"

Elle shrugged. "They're a nice reminder, I guess."

"Okay." I took another sip of my espresso. I had absolutely no idea what to think of all this. Maybe I didn't even need to, it wasn't my business anyway. "Suit yourself, then."

"Though I'm more disappointed by the fact I still couldn't scare you away from me," Elle said, but there was a huge grin lighting up her entire face, so I filed it off as sarcasm.

Still, I had to admit, "Rest assured, I am going to stop pestering you."

"You are?" Elle's eyebrows shot up.

"Definitely."

"I didn't take you as the easily giving up -type."

I smiled at that. If Elle was worried about shocking me enough for me to run from her little rope activities, she would be sorely mistaken. "I'm not. And I'm not exactly giving up—I still want you to become a singer for Ortega Records."

Elle tilted her head to the side and tapped her bottom lip with her index finger, before squinting her eyes at me. Adorable.

"Then what do you mean?" she asked.

"I'm going to let you think about it for a while. You already promised, didn't you?"

"I think I did," Elle said, and took another sip of the tea.

"What, are you going to miss me?"

Elle rolled her eyes.

"I'll take that as a yes." I smirked, earning another incredulous look from Elle.

The truth was, that because I knew Elle a bit better, I couldn't bring myself to be quite as aggressive with this as I'd been so far. I wanted her to want it, not the other way around. The last thing I wanted these days was to force her into it. Fame could also be quite scary, and not at all as glamorous as the media made it out to be.

I was, however, going to miss her passive-aggressive replies dearly.

My brain reminded my heart that I'd been blowing up her phone and invading her life strictly because of business, and definitely not because I wanted to spend time with her and learn more about her. Nope, that was not my intention at all. This was strictly about business. Yes.

Yet, somehow, I still couldn't get the taste of her lips off mine.

I didn't even realize I'd been staring at her lips until she yawned and covered them with her well-manicured hand.

"I guess I should leave you for today, at least," I said, though I didn't mean one word. All I wanted was to throw her in my backseat and drive her to my house where I could—

"I told you I would be tired after this, didn't I?" Elle said, and yawned again.

"You did," I said, and threw the rest of my espresso down my throat before standing up. The slight burn was a welcome distraction, to be completely honest. "Let me handle the bill and I'll walk you home."

"No need, I live literally around the corner," Elle said, and stood up too.

"I insist."

"Of course you do."

I was sad I didn't get to see another eyeroll she was definitely giving me, since I was already heading towards the counter. I was totally about to miss those too—the eyerolls. And the way she clicked her tongue. Or smacked her cotton candy tasting lips.

To my convenience, paying for our coffee and tea didn't require any brain activity. Otherwise, I would've been completely screwed. Elle's mere presence made me fall right down to the intelligence level of a caveman.

We thanked the staff and exited the café. Elle wasn't lying when she said she lived around the corner—we were at her building's door in 30 seconds max. I was about to panic. I didn't want to part with her yet, but even walking very slowly didn't help since Elle charged forward and I was left behind.

"I had fun today," I said when she was about to walk up the couple of steps to reach the building's entrance. It was a desperate attempt to spend a second or two more in her presence.

"I did too," Elle said, and turned to give me a small smile. "If you want, you can join us another time too."

"Sure."

"Bye Cam, see you," Elle said, and turned to face her door again.

My hand acted with its own will when it grabbed Elle's elbow. "Wait, would this be counted as a date?"

Elle's eyes widened. "I suppose it could. Why? You want to take me up?"

I yanked her closer by her elbow, so close our chests met. My fingers lingered for a second too long that was appropriate as I brushed a blond strand behind her ear. "No, I can leave that to José this time. But I was wondering if this date was as successful as the last one?"

When my hand landed on the side of Elle's neck, her skin burned.

She cast her eyes down before replying, "I think it was even better," and immediately sucked her lower lip partially in.

I took my chances and brushed my thumb below her bottom lip. "Does that mean I've earned another kiss?"

"Mmhm," she mumbled before parting her mouth.

It was all the permission I needed, but I still took my time. She all but melted against me when I grabbed her waist and pulled. Her face only got more beautiful the closer it came. I gladly admired her high cheekbones, the long lashes that framed her eyes as they fluttered closed, and the most perfect arch of her brows.

But once her hot breath tickled my lips, I had to close my eyes too, to brace myself for the taste. This time, it was honey, however. Sweet, sugary honey. I wanted to lick those pillowy, soft lips, to make the taste last longer, but ultimately kept myself in check.

I was not even supposed to kiss her in the first place. Again.

Which was the unfortunate thought that made me pull away from her, despite my heart beating so incredibly fast against my ribcage that I thought it was about to bang right through it.

"Thank you for today," I said, and took a step back.

Slowly, as if coming down from a trance, Elle opened her eyes.

"Um, yeah. Thank you too," she said, and pointed her thumb towards her entrance. "I guess I'll get going, then?"

"Yeah, see you around."

"See you," Elle said, and hopped up the stairs, then past José who was already keeping the door open, and disappeared into the corridor.

I swore I almost saw a hint of a sparkle on José's otherwise stern demeanor when our eyes met, just as he nodded my way before closing the door. I turned around and walked the short distance to my car that was parked on the side of the road with light steps. Only once I was already seated in the driver's seat, holding the steering wheel, did the full weight of what I'd done hit me.

I deflated like a balloon and hit my forehead against the top of the steering wheel.

"Ow."

Unfortunately, hurting myself helped exactly nothing and the guilt started to dwell on my stomach. At this rate, I was only going to hurt both Elle and myself. I didn't care much about the latter, but Elle didn't deserve this. And I didn't deserve her.

Yet, luckily, even if there was nothing I could do to erase my past less-than-acceptable behavior, there was still something I could do to prevent turning this whole thing from bad to worse. It was time to stop conspiring, at least. With my breath hitching to my throat, I picked up my phone and found Zoe's number in record time.

"This better be important," were the words with which she picked up the call.

"Listen," I said, going straight to business. "I want you to delete that video of Elle singing at your wedding."

"What do you mean?" she asked.

"I don't feel like pressuring her into this anymore."

"Oh my fucking God." Zoe's voice was all whiny.

"What?"

"You fell for her, didn't you." It was not a question, but a defeated sounding statement.

"I did not," I said, but the silence on the other end of the call suggested I didn't sound as believable as I wanted to sound, so I added, "I might've kissed her, but that's it."

"Cam…" Zoe's voice started to sound somewhat desperate.

"Twice."

"Unbelievable." I could see in my head this habit of Zoe's; pinching the bridge of her nose and shaking her head.

"What? As far as I recall it was your idea to treat this as dating."

"I can't believe I have to explain this to you, but I didn't mean it literally."

"What's done is done. Now delete the video for me and we'll never talk about its existence anymore, and if Elle someday wants to join Ortega Records it'll be on her own terms."

"I hate to say this at the brink of your wonderful love story, but it might be a little too late for that perfectly happy ending you've clearly planned."

"What do you mean?"

"The clip is already out there. I even had a couple of influencers share it, so it's already making rounds."

"In other words, *estamos jodidos*."

"Pretty much. Well, at least you are fucked," Zoe said, and took a deep, deep breath. "Believe me, you're the first one I'm going to throw under the bus if shit's about to hit the fan, considering Elle's best friend is my wife."

"Yes, save your marriage," I agreed. "I'll figure something out."

What that something was, I had absolutely zero idea.

MAN'S ANSWERS

Come Monday morning, no amount of coffee could've possibly woken me up at all.

"Rough weekend?" Irene asked right away, when I crashed on my office chair like a moldy, tired sack of potatoes.

I couldn't really blame her. At least in the morning when I'd last glanced at a mirror, I'd looked like a ghost.

"You have no idea."

It was already usual for me to be tired for a day or two after a session with Takaki-san, but this time there was the added excitement of Cam being there too. I'd even been on such a high adrenaline rush I'd agreed to go for a small coffee date with him afterwards. The man was growing on me at an alarming speed, even if I knew he was mostly interested in me professionally. I had no idea what the kisses were about. Maybe they were there just to give me false hope.

"In other news, have you seen the—" Irene asked, but Greg cut her off.

"Elle, a minute please," he said, and nodded towards his office.

He had this frown that somehow twisted his entire ugly face rather than just his forehead.

"Hold that thought," I mouthed to Irene and followed Greg right away.

What was even the point of trying to figure out what I'd done wrong this time? It was obvious I'd already fucked around and was about to find out, anyway. This scumbag couldn't leave me alone.

Once I entered Greg's office, he sat on his throne-like office chair, laid his hands on the table, and crossed his fingers, then took a deep breath. "You know SCRN Inc cares a lot about its public image."

I swallowed the urge to strangle him for no apparent reason, other than him being an obvious douche. I was, after all, one of the most public employees of the entire company, so one could say I did know a thing or two about SCRN Inc's public image. Somehow, I still forced this sweetest, most oblivious smile on my face—no need to lower myself to Greg's very low level. "Of course."

"Then care to explain this?" he asked and clicked a button on the remote for the flat screen on the wall.

It directly opened a video, of which I was apparently the main star. Greg pushed play, and I got to hear me singing in Jemma's wedding. Hearing my own voice from an outside source never got old, it was still very cringey. Even after having gone through hours and hours of voice training. I glanced behind and cursed at myself for leaving the door open, since now the entire office could hear my singing as well.

Once Greg hit pause, I breathed in, relieved that the sound had stopped, and replied, "It's me, singing at my best friend's wedding."

"And let yourself be filmed?"

"People usually do film at weddings." I didn't see the point of this entire conversation, to be honest. Still, I left out the part that no one was supposed to film at Jemma's wedding, at least at the ceremony—I figured it wouldn't have helped my case a lot either way. Besides, this was a private matter, not something Greg should be concerned about either. It had nothing to do with SCRN Inc. Not that I was exactly pleased to have found out that someone had leaked a video of me singing at my best friend's wedding. Nor that it was famous enough of a video for Greg to find it. Still, it wasn't his concern.

"I'll let it slide this one time, if you make sure this video doesn't exist by tomorrow morning," Greg said, and rubbed his neck tiredly as if he'd been up all night.

I still wasn't sure what was wrong with the video but shrugged anyway. It's not like I could do much for a random video online, but I didn't particularly like it either, so I was for sure at least going to try to get rid of it. Besides, this really didn't give Greg grounds to fire me or anything, no need to take the whole thing to heart.

What I wasn't prepared for, was what Greg had in mind next.

"Consider this a warning; you're fired for the next one," Greg continued. "We can't afford have your trans voice circulating the internet—"

"My *what* voice, exactly?" My hands balled into tight fists, enough for me to dig my nails in to my palms. I'd taken a lot of shit from Greg, but this must've been his peak moment. I shook from absolute, burning rage. Trans voice? What the hell did that even mean? Screw the video, I suddenly had much more important things to be pissed about.

"Don't take it personally, it's a company policy."

Sure, a policy I'd never heard of. "So let me get this straight, this company is absolutely fine with using me as the 'quota queer' but my trans voice—" I did the air quotes. "—is too much?"

"Calm down, Miss Wright," Greg said. "Don't make me call security."

I laughed right in his face from the bottom of my heart. Security? Really? "No need, I'll see myself out. And you don't have to fire me either—I quit."

I stomped out of Greg's office. There was this faint something about me being obligated to leave a two weeks' notice, which I ignored completely. Greg could keep his fucking two weeks' notice. Instead, I strode directly to my cubicle, only to grab my purse and throw some personal items in an empty print paper box I found under my desk.

"What's going on?" Irene asked, her eyes all wide.

"I quit."

"You what?"

"I quit. Fuck Greg." I shook my head before muttering with a much quieter volume, "Trans voice? What in the actual fuck…"

"Don't forget me when you're famous," Irene said, and leaned back in her chair. "I didn't know you could sing that well."

"Great, so you've seen the video too." I was about to growl in frustration.

"Honey, I don't think there's one person in the entire building who hasn't seen it; Susan sent it to the group chat last night."

Susan? As in, my ex-boss? God I missed her. Too bad, I'd already rage quit.

"Whatever. I'm off."

I back-hugged Irene, whispered a quick "Call me later," in her ear and waltzed to the lifts, took one to the ground level and stomped all the way outside.

The air tasted like freedom once I stepped onto the street. I took it in deep and let the morning sun glare directly on my face for a hot second before briskly walking in any direction my feet took me. I didn't have a specific destination in mind, I wanted to get out, to get somewhere other than SCRN Inc and especially away from Greg.

I couldn't quite believe I'd rage-quit my first ever actual full-time, adult job, that paid all the bills and more. The tears burned behind my eyelids, but I absolutely refused to give Greg that much power over my emotions. This was exactly the irresponsible shit I'd tried to avoid doing when turning down Cam's offers, but here we were either way.

As I walked, the realization dawned upon me. It was like my world had crumbled from under my feet. Apparently with my "trans voice" I didn't pass as cis as much as I'd thought. I no longer had the job that fed me, and moreover, it hadn't been exactly as enjoyable as before once Susan was gone.

Then all this time, what was the point of turning Cam down anyway?

I ended up at the edge of the park only a few blocks from SCRN Inc. With a sigh, I sat down on a bench and set the box beside me, before picking up my phone. I stared at the blank screen for a while, feeling like I'd gotten right back to square one of adulthood.

24 and jobless. I was barely even out of college. I had a grand total of zero connections so far—I'd only gotten the job I had at SCRN Inc through an internship and because Susan took a liking to me for whatever reason—and because of my transness. Yes, ironically enough as that detail also got me rage quit.

Eventually, I turned the screen on and started browsing job listings. God I hated job hunting. I knew that with my little semi-public hobby with ropes, I had a fairly limited selection anyway. The ones I saw at first glance, either offered shit hours or crap pay. It seemed hopeless.

"Hey, aren't you the singer who's going viral?"

I lifted my eyes off the screen to meet this, uh, *very* flamboyant man...boy. I had no idea what his age was, maybe something between 15 and 30, but I did very much notice he was quite literally sporting a pink sparkling crop top paired with the shortest mini shorts I'd ever seen in my life and heels. "Um, I guess?"

"*Gurl,* you sing, like, *really* well," he snapped his fingers and clicked his tongue. "Slay."

Somehow, miraculously, I managed to mumble a "Thank you," instead of watching after him with mouth hanging open as he sauntered off, heels clacking against the asphalt.

I guess it still rang true that the gays knew all the new things first. This whole encounter circled my scattered thoughts and brought me right back to Cam's offer. "Making me a star" or whatever. Even the idea of me being famous tickled me. I snorted. Yeah, that was very far-fetched.

Somehow, I still ended up finding the clip Greg had shown me from the wasteland of the internet. I had a ridiculous number of views. Like, well over a million, and it had only been uploaded last Thursday. The video was total crap, all shaky and shit, and hearing my own voice still irked me out quite the lot...but there was something there that shifted within me when I suffered through the entire video I hadn't even known existed half an hour ago.

I couldn't quite explain what changed. Maybe it was Cam's persuasion finally catching up to me. Maybe it was my annoyance over Greg getting all offended over my voice. Maybe it was the video. Or that boy who'd already disappeared around the corner.

Maybe, just maybe, I could give this whole singing thing a chance.

I pulled up my contacts and browsed "I" for "Irritating Prick" and hit call.

Cam answered after only a couple of beeps. "This is a first; Miss Elle herself called me and not the other way around. I'll have you know I ended an entire meeting because for you, *nena*. What's up?"

I ignored all his bullcrap and went straight to the point. "Do you still want to sign me?"

"Why, of course I do," he said, and I could almost hear the sappy sweet contentment from his voice. I bet he'd waited for this exact call.

"With all the previously offered perks included?"

"Naturally," he said. I could almost imagine him relaxing in his office chair and twirling a pen.

"Then, I want you to answer a few questions carefully, and *do not* screw this up, okay?" I still wasn't convinced about any of this, but I had to try.

"Shoot," he said, still at ease.

I took a deep breath. *Here we go I guess.*

"Did you film the video?" First things first.

"What video?" he asked, his voice ringing false innocence rather loudly.

The disappointment hit fast and hard. "Incorrect."

Cam laughed. "Oh, *that* video."

"Mhmm. I know you've seen it." How could he not? There was a ridiculous number of views on that video and one would assume a record label big shot kept in touch with what was going on in the world of social media. "Now answer me, did you film it or not?"

"No, I didn't film it. I respected the brides' wishes to not have the ceremony recorded."

"Correct," I said, and let my stiffened shoulders drop. Cam had been so close to fucking up upon the first question alone, that it wasn't even funny. "Now, did you upload it or distribute it?"

"No."

Cam's "no" sounded surprisingly sincere, but… I wasn't dumb.

"Do you know the person who did?" I asked.

"Yes."

"Are they on your payroll?"

"Technically speaking, no."

"And actually speaking?"

There was a moment of silence before Cam answered my question. "It was…a close partner to Ortega Records, but no, not someone directly working for me."

"So Zoe."

"Mmhm," he mumbled. It wasn't a yes or a no, exactly, but I could let this one slide. It wasn't that important who exactly it was, I bet they were in this together somehow anyway.

"Is it possible to make the video not exist?"

"The original—sure. But the way it has spread like wildfire, it'll be on the internet forever. In fact, we could even use it—"

"Careful now, Cam," I stopped him mid-sentence. "I'd like to preserve my innocence for a little while longer."

Cam only chuckled as a reply.

"Final question," I said, and prepared for the worst. "Did you somehow encourage, with incentives or otherwise, for this person to upload or distribute the video for the sake of having an advantage over me?"

"Elle, *mi sol*," Cam said, and stayed silent for a second. He was totally using the Spanish thing to soften me up and I hated to admit that it was working.

"Cut to the point, please," I pleaded.

"If you want me to pass this test of yours, it might be better if I skip this question entirely."

"So that's an affirmative; you did encourage it."

Cam didn't reply.

"Fine," I said, and briefly gritted my teeth together. I couldn't believe I was about to do this. This whole signing for Ortega -thing had red flags all over it, but I was about to ignore every single one of them. What was it with this day that made me decide on life-altering choices every fifteen minutes?

"I'll sign with you. But so you know, you're on thin fucking ice, Mr. Ortega."

I smashed the "end call" button a little harder than I'd planned. This must've been the weirdest Monday morning in my entire life. At the very least, it was the most mentally taxing one.

I picked up the box and headed home. Surely, Cam was about to text me the details anyway, even without me asking for them. He was annoying like that. It was also annoying how much my mood shifted for the better by hearing his husky, deep, and sexy voice over a goddamn phone call.

FATHER'S CHALLENGE

However long I stared at them, I couldn't quite believe the numbers I saw on my laptop's screen. They were way too low for what I'd planned for Elle's budget. In fact, the numbers were lower than the budget of any other Ortega Records artist this or last year. It was absurdly sucky.

Papá.

It *had* to be his doing. Carlos Ortega could be a very irritating man whenever he damn well pleased. Apparently, this was one of those times.

I'd finally gotten Elle to promise to sign with us and this was the budget he'd come up with? It barely even covered the advance I'd promised Elle for the debut album. If I proposed this budget to Elle, I was sure I would have to get back to crawling at her feet to get her to work with me.

This was exactly why I wanted Dad to retire. It was like a slap on my face that dropped me right back to earth from the euphoria of finally getting the "yes" from Elle. I would have laughed if I wasn't so pissed. I printed the budget sheet and strode into *Papá's* office on the other end of the floor and smashed it on the table in front of him, completely ignoring the fact that he was on the phone.

"I'm afraid I'll have to call you back," he said, toying with his pen. "Cameron looks like he's about to blow up. Yes, have fun on your honeymoon trip. Say hi to Jemma for me."

I didn't even bother to wait until he'd ended the call properly, only tapped the paper with my index finger. It sounded like he'd been talking to Zoe, anyway. "What's this?"

"Sit down," he said, and brushed back his deep brown hair.

I obeyed—not because I wanted to, but because I already knew that I needed to pick my fights with the old man carefully. If I wanted to get hung up on this, I wouldn't even have a chance to try to fix this budget thing.

"Now," Dad said, and leaned back in his chair. "What happened to 'hello, how are you?' It's been too long since we've had an actual conversation, don't you think?"

I stayed silent, feeling like a bomb was ticking inside me and it would detonate and blow this entire building up if I opened my mouth.

"Fine, I'll do the talking then. First of all, congratulations for acquiring Elle, she truly seems to be a talented singer."

I lost it. "Then what's with this ridiculous excuse of a budget?"

"I had a great chat with Zoe the other day and I gathered that you've been a little *obsessed* lately," *Papá* said, and stood up, then turned to stare out the window at the back. "Don't you think you're taking this too personally? This is business, after all. While I'm all about passion, there needs to be a certain amount of rational thinking involved as well. At the moment, it seems like you lack the latter."

I cursed Zoe to the deepest pits of hell for ratting me out. "Believe me, *Papá*, I am the one who's thinking rationally here. This budget is absolutely useless!"

"Challenge," he said. "It's a challenge. It's about time you take one. Lizette spoiled you way too much."

"Don't bring *Mamá* into this." My teeth ground together so hard my jaw hurt.

"Cameron," Dad said, his voice oozing finality. "You have two options. Either we do it my way, with a minimal budget. Elle will release an album that will be forgotten within a year, unless you miraculously get an organic hit on it. Even in that case she'll end up a one-hit wonder because we won't do another album. *Una pena…*"

"The other option. I want the other option."

"Well, if you're really as sure about Elle as you've been saying, you'll gladly invest your own money on her debut, and I'll double whatever you can scrape together. We'll actually get to see if Elle makes it, and if she does, she's going to pay back both of our investments. I will be happy to handover Ortega Records to you and retire."

I squinted at him. My own money? It felt like a trap. In order to scrape together at least a semi-decent budget, I would have to liquify all my assets and possibly even bind my house for an insane loan. If someone was taking this personally, it was *Papá*; he could very much afford it even without all this extra bullshit. *Ortega Records* could very much afford it. Why the heck would I need to invest my own money?

Then again, if this was what it would take to finally properly run this business, I'd totally take it.

"If she still doesn't make it," *Papá* said, and turned around to face me, his eyes all twinkling as if he was having more fun now than he'd had in the past decade. I hadn't seen him this, um, *high-spirited,* in ages. "At least you can say you've given her a fair chance."

"Deal." This was going to be a total headache, but hopefully a lucrative one.

"Wonderful!" *Papá* said, and clapped his hands together. "Now that we've got that settled, would you care to join me for lunch?"

"No thank you," I said, and stood up, almost knocking the chair over in the process. "Thanks to you, I'll be busy calling the banks until Elle arrives to sign the contract…" I checked my wrist watch. "…in half an hour."

Crap.

I didn't stay to hear *Papá's* protests. Look, I knew he was probably just lonely—had been since *Mamá* had died two years ago—but him getting on my nerves every chance he got, didn't exactly help his case. Especially at work, he was all about testing me. I bet he'd relax a little after retirement. In fact, I was counting on that.

Which meant I really needed this Elle thing to work. I needed it to work magnificently. She needed to become an entire superstar, and goddamn fast. The full weight of the hell I'd signed up for hit me when I crashed on my office chair and buried my face in my hands. *Papá* and his insane plans.

For the first time since the Saturday of Zoe and Jemma's wedding, I had the tiniest amount of doubt. After all, I was risking my entire life for this, for Elle. I happened to like my life. I'd made it comfortable.

"Elle is here," my secretary called out from the threshold.

I snapped to look at the door. Elle was early. I took a deep breath and straightened my back. There was no point in stalling, anyway. What was done, was done—I'd already agreed with *Papá.* "Let her in."

Then…something magical happened. All my doubts and worries evaporated when Elle appeared at the door, a smile on her pink glossed lips, looking like a goddess. I barely held myself back from getting up, grabbing her in my embrace and devouring those juicy lips, before taking her to my house to continue far further than merely kissing. Her outfit consisting of pretty much only a miniscule crop top and some faded blue, figure hugging jeans, surely didn't help with my noble quest of keeping my unwanted feelings for the woman in check.

I made the right decision. She deserved the world, and I was dead set on giving it to her. I would've sold my entire fortune three times over if that's what it took to let her debut as a singer.

"Hi," Elle said, and took a step in, then glanced down. "Is there something wrong with my outfit?"

I blinked and forcefully tore my eyes off her.

"Hi," I greeted back. "And no. It's alright. Please, sit," I said, and gestured at the chair in front of my desk.

"Thanks," she said, and sat down. "So, how do we do this?"

"Did you go through the contract with a lawyer?"

"Yes," Elle said, and dug out a pile of papers from her purse, before laying them on the desk in front of me. "Here. Though, I'm not sure why you insisted on it, because it cost a literal fortune for him to say it's surprisingly fair and generous. There's only a couple of suggestions—mostly nitpicking on words used. He marked them in red."

I took the papers and started browsing. "Lesson number one; go through every single paper with a lawyer before signing anything. Even papers you get from me."

"Noted."

Elle was speaking the truth—there was barely anything that needed to be changed. "Okay, these all seem good. I'm going to change these few things quickly and then we can both sign. Is that alright with you?"

"Yeah, I kinda need the signing bonus," Elle admitted and evaded my eyes. "I might've rage quit and the lawyer cost a lot. Like, all my savings."

My heart sank to the bottom of my stomach and I put down the papers. In the end, I was still Elle's future boss, and I had to think about the company's future too… as well as manage Elle's expectations. Not to even mention I'd agreed to put my entire life on the line for her to debut. "You do realize you won't be able to rage quit this, right?"

"Yes, I—" Elle said, and stopped mid-sentence for a moment. "I am committed to this. My substitute boss really got on my nerves. He's a bit of a transphobe."

"Elle, this might be me shooting my own leg. Plus, I'm only going to say this once and because I genuinely care about you; in this industry you're going to meet a lot of transphobic people. I will make damn sure there won't be one in Ortega Records, yes, but I physically can't protect you from the whole entire world, even if I madly want to."

"I know, I'm—"

"And while we are only doing a one album deal at first, once you're famous, that's it. There's a chance you'll be famous forever, whether you like it or not. I need you to be in this 100% or not at all. Time to choose."

It looked like my words really hit something in Elle, because she fell completely silent and turned stiff as a statue. My heart clenched—did I scare her off right when I was about to get her? Maybe I should've stayed silent.

I definitely should've stayed silent.

Yet, there was nothing else to do now than wait for Elle's reply, my heart aching and crippling fear growing inside me. I wasn't sure how much time passed, but the seconds seemed to stretch into minutes, and the minutes seemed to stretch into hours. By the end of it, I was 99% sure Elle was going to back off.

"I'm aware of what this means to my life," Elle finally said, and my breath hitched in my throat as I waited for the rest of it. "But I am going to do this. I want to do this. Hell, if you no longer want to sign me, I'll find someone else who will."

I exhaled, and a smile tugged the corners of my mouth up.

"Don't you dare go find someone else; you're mine now. Well, soon, anyway."

As I pulled the laptop closer to me in order to get on with the changes to the contract, I saw Elle relaxing in her chair. Good. It meant I could relax too.

Getting the documents done didn't take me long at all, and soon I had the entire thing printed in two copies—one for me and one for Elle. I signed both first. There was no need to hesitate anymore. Then, I handed them over the table. "Here you go."

Elle picked up one of the contracts and started reading through it without saying anything. I told myself I was glad to see her taking this seriously enough to read through them once more, but in reality I was totally enchanted by her face of concentration. She had this adorable wrinkle between her eyebrows as she read through the papers. She also poked her cheek with the back end of the pen from time to time.

Once she was done, she didn't hesitate either. She unceremoniously signed the papers and then it was official. She was mine. Or Ortega Records's, but I wasn't about to start nitpicking. That tiny annoying voice in the back of my head that tried to tell me I also wanted her to be mine in some certain other ways too, I forcefully silenced. This was definitely not the right time for that. Especially after my conversation with *Papá* earlier—I wanted to prove him wrong, not right.

Yes, I was definitely not taking this personally at all.

"So, what happens now?" Elle asked as she handed me my copy of the contract. "I magically learn how to do all this and pop out an album within like a month?"

I chuckled and moved my copy of the contract aside. "Not quite. My rough plan was to publish one or two singles next spring, and then the album in the beginning of summer."

Elle's eyes widened. "That's months away."

"These things take time. Especially because you don't have any songs in your back pocket, now do you?"

"No, I don't." Elle cast her eyes down.

I started counting with my fingers. "Soon, you're going to have to decide on a management company—I suggest Zoe's Fame Factory—but it's really up to you. Then, you need lots of training, both vocal and dancing, maybe an instrument—"

"Wait, I'm going to dance, too? I thought this was about singing?"

"If you want to put on a proper show one day, then yes. I do recommend it."

"Crap."

"Don't worry, I'll get you the best teachers."

"You better because I've got two left feet."

The scenes from Takaki's studio flashed before my eyes. Just the bodily coordination needed to pull that off, had been enough for me to not believe it at all. "Nonsense."

"Lucky for you, I do like to dance," Elle said, "I just don't know how to."

I nodded, then continued with my counting. "Then we need to decide on a theme and concept for the album and merchandise, find or compose the songs, record them, film music videos… It wouldn't hurt if you could score a sponsor or brand deal even before that, maybe start building a social media presence—"

There was one of those cartoony lightbulb moments going on above my head, and I snapped my fingers. "I have an idea—do you have time now?"

"I was supposed to celebrate this with Jemma briefly today before they fly off to Bahamas the day after tomorrow, but I guess I'm not in a hurry before the evening—"

That was all I needed. I stood up, apparently startling poor Elle in the process as she jumped an inch in her seat. I ignored it and grabbed her elbow. "Let's go."

"To where?" she asked as she stumbled up.

"You'll see," I said, and started dragging her out of my office.

PRODUCER'S OPINION

Funny how only two days prior, I'd found myself in a whole pit of despair, having rage quit my first actual adult job with absolutely no idea what I was going to do with my life. That was all only for this fine, random Wednesday to come, when Cam dragged me inside an honest to God recording studio. I stared at the microphone with the pop filter through the window of the mixing room. It felt like I'd been transported into a movie or something. Like, there was no way this was real life.

Everything happened so fast. One moment I was in Cam's office, having just signed the contract, with Cam rapid firing me with all the scary things I would have to do to make this rather dreamy career change happen. Next second, I'd found myself here.

"So, what exactly are we doing here?" I asked. "I don't think I magically conjured up an entire song in the span of two minutes. I'm a fast learner, alright, but I'm not a miracle worker."

"I figured that we could record a proper studio version of *Whisper*," Cam said.

Oh. The song I sang at Jemma's wedding. "Um, okay?"

"That way, I can get an idea of what we need to work on and what you're capable of. Then you could work with Zoe—er, with the management company of your choosing—on how to use the song. It can be like a video, some kind of introduction. Something that informs people you've now gotten yourself a record deal. I bet with the attention the secretly-filmed clip is getting already, you could even score a brand deal—"

"Hold on a minute." My brain was turning into mush. "Slow down. Brand deal?"

"You know, when they pay you for using their clothes publicly, for example."

"Yes, I do know what a brand deal is, but…" It felt so incredibly far-fetched for a nobody like me. "Nevermind. So how are we going to do this?"

"We happen to have a few unreleased remixes of the song," Cam said, and fired up the computer. "I figured we'd listen through them, you pick your favorite, and we record some new vocals over them."

Sounded simple enough to me. I crashed on the couch at the back.

"Alright. Hit it."

"Just a minute," he said, browsing some kind of cloud service. "Ah, here, found them. The first one is very modern pop if I remember correctly."

Cam hit play, and the room filled with music. At first, I was amazed by the sound quality. It was out of this world. But when

I really concentrated on the track with no vocals, I wasn't very impressed.

Once we were past the chorus part, I said, "I mean, it's nice and all, but it's kind of, um, plain."

"Yeah, it's pretty basic," Cam said, nodding. "This one is on the other end of the scale. Slow, with sort of a heavy beat. Definitely not my personal favorite, but it's different."

Now that one, it really hit something within me. The tempo was—how should I put it—a perfect love-making pace. It captured the essence of the original version I'd heard a thousand times, and loved, but magnified the feel ten-fold. It was heavy, like Cam said. A mix of acoustic and machine induced bass, some cello, even some violin sprinkled in the background. The basic guitar and drums didn't take too much space away from the classical instruments, but were there when needed when the song built up the tension for the bridge before the last chorus.

"I really like this," I mumbled, having closed my eyes and leaned back on the couch, completely taken into another world by the track.

"Interesting, but let's hear my favorite first before making any rash decisions."

I was a little sad to part with the track but nodded anyway.

Cam hit play on another track and I couldn't help but admit it was beautiful. However, I felt like it was missing something. It was mostly a piano arrangement, with a very underwhelming band in the background. There was barely any build up towards the end, and it was so simple I felt like it relied heavily on the vocals, and had no flavor of its own.

"This is your favorite? Really?" My eyebrows drew together.

"Yes. I love it," Cam said with a dreamy look on his face. "Haven't found the right vocalist for it, but I bet you could do it. What do you say?"

"Nah, I don't like this as much as the previous one," I said, thinking of how I should put it. "It's beautiful, but not quite…well, it's a little sappy. The song's supposed to be sexy. It's got all the wrong flavors. Too sweet instead of spicy and hot."

Why Cam looked hurt, I had no idea.

"The song is not supposed to be sexy," he said. "It's everything but sexy. It's supposed to be this tender, sweet, epic love song."

"Sweet? Tender?!" I wanted to laugh. "Oh, come on! Have you actually listened to the song? The lyrics?"

Obviously songs were supposed to be interpreted by the listener, but this time I was inclined to say Cam was entirely wrong. I'd always thought of it as sexy, at least more than cheesily romantic, as Cam seemed to see it.

"*You're the one who can bring me heaven,*" Cam quoted. "*'Together we'll make the world ours.'* It's a song that is regularly played at *weddings*. You should know this too, as you sang it at Zoe's."

"*Make the cold night soon disappear,*" I countered. "*'Your fierce, warm touch, it melts the night away…'* I mean, we can go on forever, but the song is sexy. Period. And weddings are sexy. As is this song."

"It's not."

"It is."

"It's not sexy, end of discussion. *Mamá* intended it to be sweet." Cam actually started to look a little pissed. "*You* are just a pervert."

Looked like I'd hit a nerve. "Then you are just biased because it's your Mom's song."

"I can still interpret songs objectively, whoever sang it first," Cam said. "I'm a professional. I've been doing this for years."

It was entirely pointless to argue with Cam, because he was not going to give up. Somehow, I still couldn't stop. He was wrong and I wanted to show him that he was. "You know what? Put the sexy version on. I'll prove to you that it's sexy. Scorching hot, even."

"Be my guest," Cam said, evading my eyes. "But it's not going to change my mind. The song isn't sexy."

"You'll see," I said, shrugging.

"Then hit it, I'll load the track. You're only getting one take for now, and if it doesn't work we're going with my version," Cam said with a smirk, pointing at the window that led to the other room, "so make it worth it."

"Trust me, I only need one take," I said, and waltzed through the door to the recording booth.

Once the door clicked shut behind me, though, my overconfidence started to fade. I mean, I had no idea what I was actually doing, or how any of this worked. But I figured I needed to open my voice up a bit so I did some random exercises I remembered from my voice training days, while I dragged a bar stool from the corner to sit in front of the microphone thingy.

When I was done, at least somewhat, I picked up an already wired-up pair of huge over-ear headphones and looked at Cam through the window.

"Listen to the track first and take whatever notes you need. Let me know when you're ready," Cam said.

I heard him in my headphones. Cool. So that's how it worked.

He messed with something on the mixing board, while I picked up some paper and set up the sheet music stand. The music started, and I focused, marking a few notes and some lyrics down. I didn't need much, I knew the song inside out already—it was one of my favorites.

After I'd listened to the song a couple of times all the way through, I looked at Cam through the window again.

He leaned over to the small microphone over the mixing table, and said, "I'm ready when you are."

I raised my hand in order to signal not quite yet and did a couple of more voice opening exercises. I didn't necessarily need them, but I needed to stall for a little while. To pull this off, I needed to get in the mood, fast. Luckily, I knew Cam was right there across the wall, so it wasn't too hard for me to imagine his hands on me, rough. Like I'd seen in my dreams ever since the night we met at Jemma's wedding.

After closing my eyes and taking a deep breath I gave Cam a thumbs up and leaned closer to the microphone. "I'm ready. Let's roll."

Singer's Invitation

When I'd come up with this version of *Whisper*, I'd instantly disregarded it as a failure. I mean I liked the sound of it, but I never thought it fit the song's mood. Who knew a couple of years later, Elle would take a liking to it.

I shook my head and opened the button of my dress shirt—I bet I would need the extra breathing room soon enough—and glanced inside the booth to see what Elle was up to. Looked like she was finally giving me the thumbs up.

"I'm ready. Let's roll," she said.

I tapped the button to turn my microphone on. "Rolling. Remember; you get only one take and that's it."

I hit play once Elle nodded as a reply.

It wasn't as much about the song being sexy in Elle's opinion that got me to insist on one take, as I'd let her believe.

It was rather the fact that I wasn't sure I could handle more than one take if Elle pulled it off. Heavens knew I was already way too much under her spell. She was literally sex on a stick, especially in that outfit I tried so hard not to stare at. At least not too obviously.

Elle made the not staring part impossible, though. She closed her eyes and swayed to the heavy beat of the song, letting her fingertips play with the silver microphone pendant I'd given her. There wasn't a second I didn't regret purchasing that—but how could I have known that the chain of the pendant was the perfect length to land in between her perfectly shaped breasts, the jewelry jiggling with Elle's movements and glimmering under the low lighting of the booth.

It was very distracting, to say the least.

But what turned out to be even more hypnotizing was the way Elle sang the song. It was nothing like back at Zoe and Jemma's wedding. It was nothing like the original version. It was nothing like the countless covers I'd heard over the years. It was completely original.

Moreover, it was possibly even better than any of the versions I'd heard before, *Mamá's* included. And it was sexy. It was sexy as hell. But I was still convinced it wasn't the song itself that was sexy, still, but Elle.

She made the song completely hers, and she was, by default, incredibly sexy. Yes. That must've been it. She hypnotized me just by existing.

I'd spent days hoping that the link, the pull, between us would somehow vanish if I kept on resisting her spells long enough. Yet, every day, it became harder and harder to resist. By this moment? It was unbearable. It was time I admitted that I wanted her. I wanted every single bit of her. All of it.

I didn't even hear the song anymore, and I couldn't focus on the lyrics as Elle sang her heart out. The only thing I could focus on was my million beats per minute, violently beating heart. That and the way blood started flowing in one direction: my cock. I don't think I'd ever been as aroused as I was then.

"Cam?" Elle's regular talking voice pierced my hazy consciousness.

Apparently, the song had already ended. How did time randomly move so fast? I cleared my throat before pressing the button to speak through my microphone, but still my voice came out husky. "Yes?"

"Now do you admit the song's sexy?" Elle asked, her eyes gleaming and her fingers slowly descending along the edge of the skimpy top's v-neck.

I shifted in my seat, hoping the movement would somehow make me feel a little less uncomfortable around my crotch. It didn't work. I was glad Elle was still inside the booth and there was an entire glass window between us, because I swear to God, I couldn't have been held accountable for the consequences if she'd sung like that in the same room with me.

"Do you do it on purpose?" I asked.

Elle raised one eyebrow. "Do what on purpose?"

"Intentionally drive me completely mad."

"Oh, I do?" Elle asked and visibly fought off a smile, before parting her legs in a very enticingly slow way. Leaning forward, she pressed one of her palms on the bar stool's middle. The position made her bosom all but fall out of the skimpy top and drew the rest of my attention to the curve of her butt. "I didn't mean to."

She totally meant to.

"Elle, I'm down to the last 2% of my patience," I said. "Don't get me wrong, it's still enough for me to back off, but please you need to tell me if that's what you want. Because forgive me God, I don't want to keep my hands off you anymore."

"Cam, do you really think you're the only one tired of waiting? Believe me, you can't even begin to imagine the twisted, inappropriate, borderline awful and unhinged things I want us to do." Elle licked the corner of her mouth and closed her eyes. "I don't want you to be able to look at me the same once we're done."

I jumped up from my chair and headed to the door. My patience…what patience? Never heard of it. I had none left, absolutely zero amount. I was surprised I caught the door before it banged loudly against the wall.

Elle's eyes widened when I barged in, and she took the headphones off.

"Cam?"

I forced myself to stop in front of her, rather than grab her in my embrace right away and touch the most inappropriate places—but man was I shaking from holding back. I did let my hand, very slowly, reach for her cheek. Her skin was burning my hand before I even touched it. Her eyes fluttered closed as she leaned the side of her face to meet my hand.

"Elle…" My voice came out rough. "I can't take this anymore. I want you. All of you, not just your voice."

She took a shaky, small breath, before whispering, "Then take me."

I let my forehead rest on hers and my hand reach for her waist to pull her closer. Our breaths mixed together in the small space between our lips, holding the full weight of our shared anticipation, our shared desire. "This complicates things, you know that right?" I said.

"I know," she breathed quietly. "And I don't care. I've wanted you since the moment we met."

Once she said it out loud, I couldn't deny it anymore; I'd wanted her too. I'd been a gone man from the moment she opened her beautiful lips and sang the first note back at Zoe's wedding.

"Please tell me I can kiss you."

Her eyes met mine. "A thousand times yes."

The tension between us finally fractured before shattering like glass under immense pressure, and I let my lips touch hers.

The kiss started innocently, chaste even, like our previous kisses. This time, though, it very quickly turned out to be the ignition to the flames that consumed us. It made our lips dance to a rather rough choreography, almost in some kind of desperate harmony of lust. I groaned in her mouth, wanting more. So much more.

As did Elle. She wrapped her arms tightly around my waist and held me with incredible strength, pressing herself against my chest, hard. Even her teeth graced my lower lip, but I couldn't have cared less in my urgency to take whatever she wanted to give me.

I also could no longer stop my hands from roaming their way all over her body—and based on Elle's response, she didn't mind. I could feel her grinding against me, even more determined the more I touched her. I let my hands linger at the arch of her waist, then on the curve of her hip, until they found themselves on her behind. She had such a perfect butt, and so much of it that even my big hands couldn't grab all of it if I tried.

So delicious. Yet, I couldn't quite let this escalate any further, as much as I wanted to. We were, after all, still on Ortega Records's premises.

It still took all my strength to pull back.

"Elle, would you mind if we continued this somewhere else?"

"No, I would not," she said, but didn't even bother to open her eyes or untangle herself from me. "The sooner the better."

"My place or yours?"

"Well, I do have a cat to feed."

I let a smile break on my lips. "How about your celebration with Jemma?"

Elle's eyes opened half-way and she smiled back at me, the expression brightening up the entire room. "She sold my contact information for pussy and a bag. She'll survive. Besides, we'll have a better time celebrating once they come back from the Bahamas."

Can't argue with that.

LOVER'S TASTE

By the time we'd gotten to my place, the overconfidence inflicted by the high I got singing *Whisper* my way had completely vanished. I fled to the bathroom with the excuse of "freshening up," but in reality, I needed a moment to gather my thoughts.

I mean, I did the freshening up as well. All douched, bushes trimmed, and all possible bits cleaned to the point they would've fucking shone in sunlight. I was polished. Yes, even the parts of me that sunshine couldn't possibly reach.

I'd also texted Jemma, and the conversation went every bit like I'd imagined it would go:

Me: Raincheck? Reason: Unexpected Dick Appointment
Jemma: Granted. Go get sum bestie!

Still, I hesitated. I didn't know why. I wanted this, I wanted him, so much it hurt. My entire skin was still heated from our earlier encounter at Ortega Records, yet I couldn't find it in me to go back to the living room.

There was also the thing regarding my…downstairs area. I mean Cam knew I was trans, but had he realized I still had a dick? He definitely only gave me 100% straight vibes. What if he ran to the hills upon realizing I wasn't 100% a woman?

I splashed some cold water on my overheated neck. I knew I was stalling, and Cam was probably getting incredibly bored as the minutes ticked by. I couldn't possibly delay this any longer.

So I took a deep breath and finally exited the bathroom. But the sight I walked in on, wasn't what I expected at all. Cam had lit up all the led candles I had scattered around my apartment—there were a lot—and turned off the lights. My living room glowed in the fake but very convincing glow of orange-yellow flames. He'd also helped himself to my liquor stash and fetched a bottle of sparkling wine. It was even in a cooler with two champagne glasses set beside it.

The sight, it took my breath away. It was definitely something the fuckboys I'd previously been with would've never even thought of doing. Not that I'd been as serious with any of them as I was with Cam.

"I, uh, I took some liberties around your place., I hope you don't mind," Cam said, and glanced at me over his shoulder just briefly before turning to stare ahead.

He was sitting on my couch with Lola at his side, purring. Cam scratched the back of the cat's neck in a way that gave me this idea that maybe I wasn't the only one nervous after all. More importantly, the gesture made his bicep flex. He'd already gotten rid of the black button-up and was now only sporting his jeans and a tank top. Suddenly that was all I could focus on.

I blinked to rip my eyes off his arm.

"No, I don't mind," I replied.

Quite the contrary. There was nothing other than gratitude I felt towards him when I carefully opened the wine and poured it into the two glasses he had set out for us. Additionally, there was no denying that I told him to make himself feel at home before I'd fled to the bathroom.

I handed one of the glasses to Cam and kept one for myself as I sat down on the couch next to him.

"Any second thoughts?" Cam asked, right before we clinked the glasses together.

"None," I started, then swallowed heavily. "But…"

"But what?" Cam asked and placed his hand on my thigh and squeezed, the gesture somehow reassuring. "Talk to me Elle, I can see something's bothering you."

I took a sip of the fizzy drink, hoping it would calm my nerves. It didn't, but it was a nice try nevertheless. I decided to spit it out, nervous or not.

"I…I still have a…well, a penis. I have a penis. It's still intact and I'm not planning on getting rid of it anytime soon. Um… That's it. I have a dick."

I swallowed the glass empty in one go, evading even looking at Cam.

After only a short silence, Cam replied, "Okay."

I snapped my eyes at him. "Okay?"

Cam shrugged. "It doesn't change anything. I still want you Elle. If you still want me, that is. But I must admit that I, too, still have a dick. I'm not planning on getting rid of it anytime soon, either. I hope that's not an issue."

I chuckled. I loved how he could do that—turn awkward situations funny. It came naturally to him, too. "I was kind of hoping you'd have one."

Cam's hand moved an inch upwards on my thigh and he emptied his glass as well, before setting it on the table. I was very much melting at his touch already, but he decided to take it a step further by grabbing my waist and scooting closer.

That was also the time the cat decided the activities were turning into something uninteresting to her, and bolted off the couch with a loud meow.

"Then what's the issue?" Cam asked, not minding the cat at all. He then cupped my face with the hand that wasn't busy at my waist, and turned me to look directly towards him.

I watched the flames dance in his brown, tantalizingly dark eyes, barely able to keep my gaze on them. "I—nothing."

"I want you so much I'm in pain, Elle. So please, if there's anything else, just say it so I can assure you whatever you're afraid of is not an issue."

His fingers danced on the skin of my waist that peeked under the crop top, slowly and barely touching. My insides ignited and started to ache with greed. I never knew a man—let alone a man with a cocky attitude like Cam—could be so gentle with his touch. However, gentle was *so* not what I was after. I wanted the roughness, the desperation I'd felt from his touch in the studio. I now knew he was capable of it.

So I grabbed his neck and smashed my lips on his without letting my brain interrupt us anymore.

Cam's response was immediate. With a guttural groan escaping from the back of his throat, he pinned me against the couch with his entire body. I could feel him everywhere at once. His lips, so slick and insistent, were on mine. His hand on my waist, and another holding me against him at my back, were so strong, so eager, it almost hurt as they slid up to meet the underside of my bra. His leg forced its way between mine and pressed against my privates.

He wasn't the only one desperate to touch the other. My insecure thoughts all but evaporated, and all I could think of was how I was going to get him naked, my skin on his skin, when I was barely capable of moving under his weight.

The couch wasn't ideal; there was little to no room to extend limbs. Not that I didn't try my hardest to get him naked by yanking his shirt up from his pants and slipping my hands underneath. But only having my hands on his feverish skin wasn't enough. I wanted my entire body tangled with his. Without a layer of clothes in the way.

I saw my opportunity when Cam moved his lips from my lips to my neck.

"Cam," I gasped in between sharp breaths. "Bedroom."

At once, his hands slipped down and grabbed my ass, then lifted me up from the couch. It was so sudden that I couldn't do much but yelp and wrap my arms around his neck and my legs around his hips. "Cam, I'm going to fall."

"Don't worry, I've got this," he said, and started walking across the room.

I wasn't the most lightweight woman to ever exist for sure, but Cam seemed to have no difficulties carrying me to the bedroom, so I let my head drop back when his lips found the nook of my neck somewhere along the way.

Cam set me down to sit on the edge of my bed and dropped to his knees on the floor. He was so tall, his eyes were only a bit below my eye level as he looked up at me, slipping his hands under my top and sliding it upwards. I helped him by raising my arms and soon, he threw the unnecessary garment at the corner of the room.

His eyes were ablaze as he intensely studied my still bra covered tits. I didn't feel awkward being exposed in front of him. Rather, I was turned on by the intensity of his gaze. It was quite something.

"You're so goddamn beautiful, *mi reina*," Cam said, the Spanish tickling something inside me despite my inability to understand it at all. Showering my collarbones and my chest with small kisses, he slowly and carefully slid his thumbs along the underwire of the bra and then let them follow the band all the way to the back, before asking with a very hoarse voice, "May I?"

It was a rather surprising question considering Cam had already seen my tits in Takaki-san's studio. Nevertheless, I nodded, and with one swift movement, my bra pretty much dropped from my body—it definitely wasn't the first time he'd dealt with a bra. I reminded myself that I was, for once, in bed with a *man* and not some loser fuckboy. He tossed it towards the exact same spot where my top had landed only a hot minute ago. I leaned back, my palms against the bed, to give him the full view and all of the access.

My nipples perked up with not much more than a touch from Cam, who all but started to worship the sight in front of him. He cupped my breasts with his hands, the touch already almost more than I could handle. Add the way his slick tongue suddenly swirled around my left, incredibly sensitive nipple, it became even more of a sensation. I could no longer hold back a moan.

"Oh, fuck," Cam mumbled against my skin before backing off.

I shivered from the sudden loss of his closeness, but instantly realized he was only taking off his shirt and not running for the hills. Moreover, I got to watch. He was in very good shape, his golden-brown skin only accentuating the definition on his abdomen. I wanted to run my hands through the light, barely there coat of hair on his chest.

So I did. I touched his chest as soon as Cam tossed his shirt to the ever-growing pile of clothes in the corner of the room. It felt incredible under my palm. The hair was somewhat coarse, but the skin underneath was firm and warm.

I didn't get to marvel at it for long though, because Cam stood up and pulled out an entire stash of five condoms still attached to each other from his jeans pocket and tossed them on the pillow before going for the button and zipper of his pants.

I had an almost all-consuming urge to run my tongue along the trail of hair that started from his navel and disappeared under the waistband.

"Let me," I said, and moved his hands aside.

I was done waiting and wanting. I needed to do, and I needed to touch.

I'd already spent way too long not touching him due to damn clothes. I wasn't about to let that go on any longer than necessary. Besides, I was curious about what I would find underneath. Thankfully, it didn't take me long to open them and yank both the jeans and underwear down with one pull.

It was perfect. The downstairs fur was trimmed fairly short but not non-existent, and his straight thick rod stood tall in full erection. I wanted to have a taste. Impatiently, I waited for Cam to step out and kick the useless clothes to the side, before asking, "Can I?"

He nodded and slid his hand through my hair.

I didn't have to be told twice. I took a condom, ripped the foil open and quickly rolled it on his length. Once that was taken care of, I grabbed his shaft and ran my tongue on the underside, before taking the whole head inside my mouth. It was big, but not so big that I had a difficult time fitting it in. I lapped my tongue around it once, which resulted in Cam groaning—music to my ears—and tightening his hold on my hair.

But that was *still* not enough. I wanted him to become desperate again. I wanted him to take me the way he damn well pleased. I wanted him to pull my hair so much my scalp ached, and ram his cock down my throat so hard I'd see fucking stars. I tried to demonstrate this by taking as much of his dick down my throat as I could, but each time I did, Cam pulled back before I even choked.

Frustrated, I yanked my head back and resorted to actual words. "Just fuck my face, Cam."

His eyes widened. "Are you serious?"

"Yes, I am," I said, with as convincing a tone as I could muster, despite the lustful haze my mind was in. "I'm a masochist and a submissive, Cam. I hang by ropes for therapy. I can handle some cock down my throat. Stop pretending to be a gentleman and fuck me."

"Then…" Cam started, his eyes ablaze once again. It looked like we were finally getting somewhere. "Can you put your hands behind your head?"

"Like this?" I asked, immediately obliging.

"Good, now cross your fingers," Cam said, barely even waiting for me to do as he said before weaving his left hand's fingers in there too, effectively trapping my hands in his. "Good girl."

I would've purred at the praise, except I yelped instead because Cam suddenly yanked our intertwined hands at the back of my head, and I all but fell to my knees on the carpeted floor. The fall was only slowed down by a little, as Cam grabbed my waist briefly with his right hand—enough for my kneecaps to not crush under my body weight. Holy fuck.

Once I got my balance back, I tested out how tight Cam's grip on my hands really was. That's when the corners of Cam's lips turned into a slight smile. "You're not going anywhere, Elle. Did you want me to fuck your face or not?"

I nodded, rather enthusiastically even. I could already feel myself slipping into the restraint high, even when there was not a single rope involved in this. Good lord, Cam was strong. My eyelids started to feel like a ton of bricks, and I let them flutter shut.

"I didn't know it was possible, but you look even prettier when you're on your knees for me." Cam said, his voice only a strained murmur. "Tongue out."

I did as I was told. Cam was surprisingly convincing with this whole thing. Only briefly, I wondered if he'd done this before, but then that thought got interrupted by two of Cam's fingers sliding on my tongue, heading to the back of my mouth, until he almost made me gag. They tasted a little salty.

"You're so ready for everything," Cam murmured with a very strange tone, almost as if he'd wondered about it out loud instead of internally. "But do let me know by shaking your head, if you want me to stop. Okay?"

I nodded again, and mumbled, "Okay," through Cam's two mouth-invading fingers. It came out all garbled, but I didn't mind making myself look like a complete fool in front of him. In fact, it kind of turned me on even more. As did Cam's ever tightening hold at the back of my head. The man could've spat on my face and I would've thanked him for it. I peeked through my heavy eyelids and saw the flames in his eyes flash a little brighter.

"Open up then, wide," he said, and I absolutely loved the way his voice sounded all kinds of strained.

He didn't give me much more of a warning before ramming his cock down my throat, so deep my eyes instantly started to water and I held down my gag reflex the best I could. Then he pulled out almost as fast as he'd plunged in. My breathing had already turned heavy and uneven, and I took in as much air as I possibly could.

"Isn't this really what you wanted, *mi hermosa?*"

Saliva pooled in my mouth, but I didn't dare to close it as Cam had said to open up. Therefore, I only nodded, and reached towards his cock on my own, taking the head in and sucking. It gave me great satisfaction to hear Cam take in a sharp breath before he groaned.

"So eager," he said, and rammed his cock all the way to the back of my throat again.

This time I couldn't hold the gag reflex as well, but Cam pulled halfway out just in time for it to not turn super uncomfortable. He continued like that, slowly at first, but picking up the pace the more he seemed to gain confidence that I wasn't about to break and I continued to show no signs of wanting to stop.

It didn't take long for my drool to pool over, and with Cam's hands still holding mine and keeping my head in place, I couldn't do much about it. First it flooded over my chin, then my throat, until it started dripping on my tits. I rarely had any spontaneous hard-ons without touching my penis these days, but to my surprise I soon found my shorts started to feel a little tight. The realization made me shift and moan on Cam's dick.

"Fuck," Cam muttered and yanked my head back, before untangling our hands. "Elle, I—I'm going to come at this rate."

Cam let go of me, and my hands dropped to my sides from pure exhaustion and I fell backwards, crashing against the side of my bed like a marionette that got its cords cut. I coughed, and lifted my heavy arm to wipe some of the drool off of my chin, only to realize it was way too much of a mess and gave up.

Instead, I croaked in between my ragged breaths, "Then why didn't you?"

"Patience, *mi amore*," Cam said, and crouched down to lift my chin up with his fingertip. "Are you still okay?"

I managed to smile, somewhat. "More than fine."

"Good," Cam said, and lifted me up from my armpits, to sit on the edge of the bed. "Got any lube around?"

Surprised, I pointed at my nightstand. I hadn't thought he'd be aware that I wouldn't get all wet on my own like other women, but I was more than happy that he'd figured that one out himself. I was not too keen on being the teacher of basic anatomy of which most men seemed to have a lacking understanding in.

Cam didn't take too much time rummaging through the drawer since it was right on top for my pathetically single nights.

"This one?" he asked, holding up the small bottle.

"Yeah."

I watched Cam set the lube bottle on the nightstand and then kneel in front of me. As he looked at me, all I wanted to do was crash on the bed, I was so exhausted. I was also coming crashing down from the high of being held almost immobile. I was such a sucker for feeling restrained.

Apparently, Cam sensed that something was going on with me. He lifted my ankle with one of his hands and laid a soft kiss on it, before looking up at me like a lost puppy. "Did I do something wrong?"

"No, I—" I started, but paused to rearrange my words. "I'm coming down from the high, that's all."

"High?" he asked.

"Yeah," I said, evading his eyes. "It's the same thing that happens with ropes. I'm sure you remember."

"So…it's a good thing?"

I sighed. "Extremely."

"Then… Do you want to continue or call it a night?"

"Continue," I said, and tried to smile. "But, you know, just don't go this soft on me in the middle of everything, and we're all good. If…if it's alright with you."

"Trust me, I'm very alright with it…if you are. I don't want to hurt you."

I almost burst out laughing, but held it in at the last fraction of a second. Hurt me? Give me a break. I was more concerned about hurting his ego—some men had very fragile ones.

"Sure," I said, and spread my arms wide open. "I'm all yours tonight so have at it!"

"Then…" Cam said, and grabbed my ankle in a tight hold. He used it to make me fall back and turn around to lay on my stomach. "Remember you asked for it yourself."

"Yeah, yeah—" I started, but then gasped instead of whatever I was going to say, because Cam yanked my shorts down to my knees with one swift movement and smacked my ass so hard it actually stung. I jerked forward, my suddenly exposed dick rubbing against the sheets. The surprise made my heart jump and breath hitch, too.

I swear that man was a mood swing and a half. One moment he was all sweet, and the next he was throwing me around like I was barely an object for him to use. I loved it. I actually loved the sweet part of him too, just not during sexy times. It was still good to know it was there.

My rambling thoughts got interrupted by another stinging slap on my ass, followed directly by Cam's hands turning soft, kneading the pain away. They then traveled up to my waist, played with my hair, lingered around until they turned harsh again. As he alternated between rough and soft touches, I was held on the edge of the bed and the edge of my sanity, without knowing what was to come next but also horny beyond imagination.

"Put your hands behind your back and stay still for me, Elle," he said, his tone the hottest version of demanding I'd heard in a while.

I couldn't have obeyed faster.

His hands slipped between my legs, played with my privates before his finger pressed against my hole as if to test the waters. I squirmed in his hold, letting out an embarrassing little greedy whine.

"Do you want something here that bad?" Cam chuckled.

Aroused, all I could manage to say was a faint, "Yes."

His hands disappeared and the bed dipped. I turned to look and noticed Cam sat next to me and reached for my back. Sure enough, he took both of my wrists in his hold, pressed them against my back, and slapped my ass again.

"Very well then, my greedy one," he all but purred as I felt lube dripping down my ass crack. I took in a sharp breath—not even for the slap, but for the coldness of the lube. I tried to arch my back to give Cam better access, but he didn't allow it.

Cam slid his free hand down towards where the lube had landed. My entire body wanted to arch to meet him halfway, to make him reach the target faster, but Cam held me still easily enough. It was like he didn't even have to make an effort.

So there I was. My hands were behind my back, ass up on the edge of the bed, my shorts still tangled at my knees keeping my legs together. I felt so exposed, so incredibly turned on, and so impatient for Cam to reach my hole with his magical fingers. He took his time.

I all but moaned when he finally slid his finger down the slit and found the pucker. All the nerve endings around the area down there lit up like a fucking Christmas tree, and I wriggled in Cam's hold. Not that it helped any. Cam started teasing me even more enthusiastically, massaging the entrance, maybe lightly pressing against it, but never slid even an inch in, before backing off and starting all over again. It was frustrating—which was most likely what Cam was aiming for.

Eventually, I couldn't take it anymore.

"Cam…please," I whined, my voice a mess and words coming out disjointed.

"Please, what?" he said, and pressed against the entrance but not enough for it to go in.

"Please, ah, just put it—" I had to take a breather in between. "—inside."

"Like this?" he asked, but didn't wait for a reply before sliding one in all the way to the knuckles.

"Ah, yes," I breathed, then bit my lip so I wouldn't whine too loudly from the sudden wave of pleasure that shook through my entire body—for a super straight looking dude like

Cam, he surely knew where the magic spot was easily enough. "More."

"More? Already?"

"Yes." *Moan.* "More." *Breath.* "Now."

"As you wish," he said, and proceeded to pull the finger almost all the way out before ramming it back in with a friend.

He started moving them in a rhythm that changed every now and then, so I never got used to the absolute firework of sensations his movement sent rippling through me. His name danced at the tip of my tongue as I tried my hardest to hold it back, my body arching as much as it possibly could under his tight hold, until I couldn't keep it in any longer.

It came out as a long, continuous whine—a desperate call— when my eyes closed involuntarily. "Cam…"

"Tell me what you want."

"More. Just more."

"I guess it can't be helped, then," Cam said, and let go of my hands. At the same time, his fingers disappeared from my ass.

I wanted to say I wanted more, not less, as I kicked off my shorts. But then Cam turned me over and started fiddling with his cock—getting rid of the old condom and rolling on a new one. To be honest, I would've been good with the same, but I did appreciate his thoroughness when it came to safety. One could not be too careful with these things I guess. I wanted his hands and cock back on me faster.

Once he was done, he looked at me and immediately scrunched his eyebrows. His lips turned into a hard line. "Are you hiding from me, Elle?"

I looked down and saw I'd hid my penis under my hands somewhere along the way, unintentionally. "I—Yes?"

His facial features softened as he leaned down and laid a soft little peck on my hand that was hiding my bits. "Would turning back around make you more comfortable?"

"No, I'm good—" I started, but swallowed the rest of the sentence as Cam laid another kiss on my hand.

Rendered speechless, I could only shiver when he then ran his tongue down my index finger until it reached what I was hiding. Hovering there, his lips dangerously close to some very sensitive parts of me, he asked, "Do you not want me to touch there?"

A surge of heat crept up my neck, and I stayed silent because I didn't have the answer for his question. But Cam was patient, almost too patient as he started kissing just about anywhere else but *there*, where I started to want him to touch the most. It drove me to the brink of insanity.

Somewhere along the way, I let my hands drop to my sides. Almost involuntarily, my hips raised at the same time, as if reaching for his lips.

However, Cam evaded me.

"Words, Elle," Cam murmured, his voice husky and desperate. "I need words."

"Y-yes," I sighed, shivering all over from pure want. "Kiss me, Cam."

That finally made his slick lips land on my shaft first, then move down at the same time his fingers started teasing my backside again. It wasn't like a blowjob, it was more like he was…giving me some oral love, not that much different from what I imagined he would've done for different kinds of parts.

It was overwhelming. So overwhelming I couldn't take it anymore and breathed, "Fuck me, Cam."

"As you wish," Cam said as his face popped up from my crotch. He flashed me a smile before starting to lather his cock with more lube. He then used the same hand to rub the leftover lube all over my parts.

To say I became rock hard, fast, would've been an understatement. I don't know how Cam managed it, but his touch was so skillful, all soft on the more sensitive places and rough on other, not so sensitive spots. It must've been a record because I was already leaking a little of love juice—well that, or it was because it was Cam, the subject of all my sweetest and thirstiest dreams ever since Jemma's wedding.

"Cam, please," I begged in between my heavy breaths. "Fuck me already."

It looked like that was what Cam had been waiting for, since he didn't waste any more time to line up his cock with my hole and plunge it right in without mercy.

I almost passed out. The pain, the pleasure, all overwhelmed me so much my eyes squeezed shut and my throat produced a loud cry.

"I didn't wait for this long to not see you come undone. Eyes open, Elle. Stay with me now."

I set my eyes on him, barely peeking through my extremely heavy lashes.

"Do you understand?"

My breath was ragged, my body a shuddering mess, but I did manage to nod.

The edges of my vision blurred as he plunged inside me over and over again, and played with my cock, until my world all but unraveled. It was like he completely broke me into tiny little pieces, chipping my existence away from the edges with each thrust, until there was nothing else left but a pure, pleasant bliss.

Even the corners of my eyes watered when I came harder, longer and more intensely than I'd come in a while, my love juices pooling on my abdomen.

Through the absolute cloud nine of my orgasm, I almost missed that Cam slid his finger through the thin clear substance and popped it inside his mouth for a taste. He even closed his eyes and marveled at it.

"What the hell are you doing?" I asked, mortified.

"What? It tastes good," Cam said, and smirked.

"Suit yourself, I guess," I replied, and covered my eyes with my arm.

My little post nut clarity was interrupted by soft lips landing on mine, and a hand yanking my arm off my face.

"No hiding, Elle. We're not done yet."

LADY'S FLAVOR

I rolled Elle inside the duvet so that only her head stuck out from the top, because our after-sex shower had turned into a during sex shower rather quickly. Now that I had all the permissions to touch her, even in exactly all the ways I damn well pleased, I couldn't not. This was a safety measure. For me. My dick could not handle another round for the night.

Elle giggled. "For the love of God, what are you doing?"

"I can't see skin, or I'll fuck you again."

"I wouldn't oppose another round," she said, her voice innocent.

"Elle, I'm an old man, you've got to cut me some slack," I said, and grabbed myself a pillow before lying down next to her. "We already did it like four times. Enough."

Elle's giggling turned into a full laughing fit.

A smile tugged the corners of my mouth up. Eventually Elle's laughter toned down, but she continued smiling through the small gap in her duvet burrito.

That smile was…something else. It sent this whole tingle through the pit of my stomach. I couldn't quite believe my luck in scoring such an amazing woman. She was quite literally the whole package. Funny, beautiful, independent, had the body of a Goddess, and was spicy in bed. How she was still single, I couldn't understand, but I damn sure wanted to change that status as soon as possible.

Her eyes were drooping yet still maintained that spark she always had, and what I'd grown to love. Why she was looking back at me with a gaze as intense as mine though, I had no idea.

"What do you see?" I asked.

Elle blinked. "Huh?"

"Why are you staring at me?"

"You're looking at me too."

"Yes, but there's hardly anything worth looking at so intensely in my face, compared to yours."

"Shut up," Elle chuckled, wriggled an arm out of the duvet burrito and smacked my side with her pillow. "I'm waiting for the twenty questions game to start."

My eyebrows drew together. "Twenty questions?"

"You know, the usual. Why do I still have a dick? Why is my cum weird? Why is there so little of it? What's with the taste of it—"

"Oh, yeah, I liked it. The taste. *So* sweet." I could still taste it on the tip of my tongue if I closed my eyes and focused. It made me want to have another round just to taste it again, so I forced my eyes back open. I was convinced my dick would actually fall off if we went for the fifth round of the night, so I couldn't really afford any more of these wild thoughts.

Elle buried her face further in the duvet burrito, until only her eyes and hair stuck out. "Shut up, I'm still mortified. The point is, aren't you even the least bit curious?"

I stuffed the pillow under my armpit and rested my temple on my knuckles. "Elle, with all due respect, I kind of *don't care*. Obviously, I'm curious, but at the same time I'm well aware that actually none of those things are my business in any possible way. Think of it this way; would I ever ask such questions from a partner with a vag?"

"That's different," Elle said.

"How? Some pussies cum—yes, even the traditional ones—and others don't. Some have a huge clitoris and others I couldn't possibly find for the life of me. Let's say I encountered one with a bigger than average labia majora, would I ask why haven't they chopped them off? Or one that comes like a geyser, would I ask why there's so much of it? Spoiler: I wouldn't. I would bury my face in it, all the same."

"But—" Elle started, but I cut her right off.

"No buts. To me, your genitalia is perfect the way it is, and if you want to do something to it later, that's your business, not mine."

"If you put it that way…"

I nodded. "More importantly, I think we need to figure out a safe word. And like, some other rules as well."

To that, Elle fell completely silent at first, then evaded my eyes. When she finally spoke, it was with a surprisingly small voice compared to her usual sassiness. "So, this wasn't like a one time thing?"

My heart all but broke at that question. "Was this a one time thing to you?"

"Not if I can help it," Elle said, possibly with an even quieter tone.

I slipped my hand under the duvet, beside her neck, and brushed my thumb along her jawline. "Don't worry, I don't do one-night stands."

"So what is this then, Cam? Are we…dating? Exclusively?"

"If that's alright with you," I said, then pulled my hand back. "Though, if you still want to continue with Ortega Records, it would be wise to date in secret at first."

"I don't know, Cam," Elle whispered. "I've kind of always been the secret to dudes. Fucked in secret and then hidden in public. Like a stain they can't get rid of."

Fuck.

"I know it's not the ideal solution, and believe me I don't want to keep this a secret either. But I can't ignore my feelings anymore. I want you. All of you. Or anything you want to give to me, I'm fine with—" I snapped my mouth shut for a second to actually think. I was rambling. "I mean, it would only be for a while until you're an established artist. And of course I'd like to introduce you to my family one day. Obviously, our closest circle can be in the loop…"

"Cam…"

"Besides, it would be for your *own* good. Like, *I'm* the stain *you* need to hide. I'm down for whatever, really—"

Elle put her index finger across my lips and did the air quotes thing with her other hand. "'*You're not like other dudes.*' Got it."

My heart sank. Had I already screwed this up before it even officially started? What had I done wrong?

Elle sighed and turned to her back, letting her finger drop from my lips. I missed her touch immediately, but realized I'd probably be better off silent.

"Poor Takaki-san, he's going to be so lonely," Elle said, and smiled.

The smile gave me new hope, but something was off and I could feel it. Also…

"What does Takaki-san have to do with any of this?" I asked.

"You'd let me see him even if we start dating?"

"I don't see why I wouldn't," I said, and thought back to the time Takaki-san said he was going to lose Elle soon. I didn't get it then, and I didn't get it now. "Though, I'm not sure you'll have the time to see him as much due to your new career, but for me, personally, it's not a problem. I mean… You're not in *that* kind of a relationship now are you? At least Takaki-san said there's nothing romantic going on between you two."

"No. I mean he's important to me in multiple other ways, but he's not my lover. It's just that all my previous boyfriends have been all weird about it, so—"

"See?" It was my turn to do the air quotes thing. "'*I'm not like other dudes,*' so could you please stop comparing?"

Elle snorted. "Fine. I'm down, I guess. It's not like I can't leave you if you do end up being a douche after all."

Good luck trying. "Yeah…"

"And whatever comes to the safeword and stuff, can we just see first where this whole thing is heading?" Elle said. "Besides, it's not like we've even strayed too far from vanilla yet."

What? "That was still considered vanilla?"

"Well, maybe there was like a little flavor in there somewhere, like some chocolate crumbs or something," Elle said, and did that head tilt thing I'd grown to adore. The one she did when she was wondering about something. "I mean it was rough, but still pretty basic."

Basic. That was basic in Elle's books. "Right."

Elle looked at me through her eyelashes in a teasing manner. "Unless you need one?

"Honestly, I don't know," I admitted. "It's not like I've ever ventured even this far off vanilla before. I'm a basic dude with basic needs, I guess. Not that it wasn't hot. I liked adding a little spice."

"Could've fooled me," Elle said, and one corner of her mouth turned into a mocking smile. "With all that bossy behavior."

"No, really. I'm a total virgin—we'll, not anymore—with kinky stuff. I only looked up some things online after you took me to Takaki-san's studio." I shuddered. "I'm telling you I'm totally not into all of the stuff, but there are some things I'd very much like to try."

"No one's into all of the stuff. And if it helps, I'm perfectly capable of saying 'no' and 'stop' if I don't like something. I wouldn't say we'd need any fancier safewords until we'd venture into actual bondage play, roleplay or like CNC."

"What's CNC?"

"Consensual Non-Consent."

"What does that even mean?"

"Rape play," Elle said, and I couldn't quite understand how she could say that in such a matter-of-fact tone.

Chills ran down my spine. "No."

When Elle fell silent, I crossed my arms across my chest to stop the shivers and continued, "I mean, not trying to kink shame, but I'm absolutely never going to engage in that type of behavior. Nope. I'm more of a pleasure kind of guy."

"Yes, I did notice," Elle said, and her eyelids drooped for only a fraction of a second until they lit up. "Ooh, but there's a variation of CNC for that too."

"How would that work?" I could not, for the life of me, wrap my head around this at all. "So many orgasms one would beg to stop? But to actually like it? Is that a kink?"

"Very much so," Elle said, and started counting with her fingers. "There's also orgasm denial, edging, post-orgasm torture…the possibilities are endless. You know that feeling when just after the orgasm, your parts are so sensitive that only a breath could take you over the edge? Then repeat that over and over and over again. The absolute bliss you could find yourself from…”

My dick hurt just from the thought alone, but to cause that for Elle…to watch her writhe in a perfect mixture of pure ecstasy and severe agony…to take her to the finish line over and over again, until she begged me to stop but then convince her to agree to it just for *one more time.*

Once I felt the pressure build in my lower abdomen, I had to admit, “I guess I can see the appeal.”

“See, not as scary as it sounds now is it?”

I laughed. “I guess not. I’d still feel better if we established some ground rules.”

Elle rolled her eyes. “Okay, fine. Have you heard of the traffic lights system?”

I think I read something about it when I did my little research.

“Green means fine, yellow means risky territory and red is ‘stop everything right now,’ right?” I asked.

Elle nodded.

“Sounds good to me,” I said. At least it was something to protect both of us with. I would never forgive myself if I went too far. But… “To be clear, I still want to take this slow.”

“Of course. To me, this kinky stuff is a welcome escape from reality. I find real life situations far more scary,” Elle said, and sighed. “Like, for example, what are we—no, what am *I* supposed to do now? Where does one randomly find music? When are we going to have time for this secret dating thing?”

“So many questions for…” I glanced at the alarm clock on the side table. “4 am. Do you ever relax?”

Not that I wasn’t thinking about the same things. Moreover, I didn’t want our time together, just the two of us, to halt right as we got to this point. Hell, I kind of wanted to keep her all for myself, even if for a little while.

"I'm entering an industry I know absolutely nothing of, and I want to do it well," Elle said. "I don't want to half-ass this…or us. But I feel like it'll be impossible to balance, somehow."

"Considering you desperately need songs to become an artist, what would you think of a week or two of a getaway?" My mind started racing with the possibilities. "We could go to my mountain cabin and work on your future hits."

Eyes all wide, Elle leaned forward. "You have a mountain cabin?"

"Yeah, upstate. Well, it's *Papa*'s, but I can use it whenever I want." I had a hunch Elle would love it, based pretty much only on my intuition. I realized I knew next to nothing about her after all apart from cold hard facts everyone else knew as well. I wanted to know the things others didn't. One more reason to take a good, needed breather from LA and actually get to know more.

"I mean, I'm intrigued… But how about the recording of *Whisper*? I know nothing about the recording process but even I can tell we're not done with that one take only, even if I did prove you wrong. Also, there's the question of management company—"

"We'll have plenty of time to record *Whisper* when we get back. You can also decide the management stuff when we come back too. We don't have to solve everything right at this second. Besides, Zoe's Fame Factory is literally the best option anyway."

"What about Lola?" Elle asked.

I completely forgot the cat. "I'm sure Dee can handle her while we're away."

"Oh, Deacon? I don't know… Is he even a cat person?"

"I think he is. If not, I'll pay him enough for him to become the biggest and most loving cat person in all of California."

Elle was silent only a little while—enough for my heart to start racing in anticipation—before giving me the answer. "Then sure. I would love to go."

I let out a breath of relief.

PLAYER'S GAME

There was something extremely hot about the way Cam drove with one hand and kept his other hand resting on my thigh. His touch made all kinds of things happen in my body that made it hard to resist asking him to stop on the side of the road to fuck and/or suck me dry. Preferably both.

It was already a miracle we made it out of my apartment without fucking each other senseless. I guess some time apart does that; Cam had been busy in the office for a few days to clear out his schedule for this thing he called a little getaway, and I had my regular Saturday thing with Takaki-san followed by a day of recovering and taking Lola to Cam's place.

Thankfully Deacon had been amazing with my rather difficult-to-handle little feline. It meant I didn't have to worry too much about her for the following…week? Or two? I'd still gotten no actual answers from Cam about what was going to happen now. I mean I'd gotten a rather significant signing bonus, so I was financially good for a few months, but I still would've liked to know.

Cam seemed to be at ease, though. I couldn't really fathom why, because one would think signing a new artist would be a risk to the company as well. I thought I'd be too busy trying to get something out to make money for the company, instead of going for a "getaway" which seemed more like a luxury holiday to me.

"What's on your mind?" Cam asked, glancing briefly at me with a crooked smile on his face, before turning his eyes back to the road.

I'd apparently fallen all silent on him. I adjusted the sunglasses that had slid down my nose and straightened my back. "I'm wondering what you expect from me now."

"Regarding business? Or personally speaking?"

"I mean…both. But let's start with business."

"You're always asking about business. So boring," Cam said, but I saw he was very much smirking. Then he tapped the navigator screen to bring it to life. "We still have almost six hours left on the road, so this is as good of a time as any to talk business. What exactly do you want to know?"

"Like, just in general. What does Ortega Records expect from its artists, and what do you expect? For example, am I still allowed to perform with Takaki-san? Is there a dress code?"

"In general, you're going to have to talk about performances and dress codes and all that nitpicky stuff with your future manager. Ortega Records doesn't really deal with that kind of stuff; we produce, publish, distribute, market and sell music. This includes stuff like making the actual album happen, everything involved with music videos, ads and official merchandise etc."

"Right."

Cam barely took a breath before continuing. "But it's the management that handles your personal schedule, books gigs, agrees on interviews, deals with performance venues, promotions, organizes fanmeets, helps with social media stuff and keeps you in check."

"Wow. Then what's left for me to do?"

"Oh, plenty," Cam said, and let out a deep laugh that sounded like it came from the bottom of his stomach. "But please don't get involved with drugs—it's always a huge mess."

It was my turn to laugh. "I wasn't planning to."

"Yes, but the temptations will be there. It's more secret than in the '80s, but all that shit is still pretty readily available in this industry. Unfortunately. Take this more like a heads up."

I nodded. "Duly noted."

No lie, I was sort of relieved. Not about the drugs thing— I was totally not about to touch any illegal substances anytime soon—but rather about the fact that it started to seem more like I wasn't completely alone in this. There would be help. Sure, I would still need to learn to actually sing, perform, dance and everything, but I wasn't about to be totally left to figure all this shit out on my own.

"And personally speaking?" I asked once I'd had my moment of wrapping my head around all of the business stuff.

"Personally speaking, there's not much," Cam said, and squeezed my thigh a little. "I guess the main thing is that I'm a monogamist. All the power to those who can deal with multiple partners—but I can't do that. I'm a possessive person, Elle. I want you all for myself, and I don't handle cheating well."

"Polyamory isn't technically cheating, though," I countered, more to tease Cam but also to correct him. "And you can still cheat if you're polyamorous. Those two aren't mutually exclusive."

"Yeah, I know." Cam squeezed the steering wheel a little bit harder. "It's just not for me and neither is cheating."

One of my eyebrows rose like it had a will of its own. "But somehow that still excludes Takaki-san, correct?"

"I'm not saying I'm unreasonable." He shrugged. "You yourself said that Takaki-san is different."

I guess I was still adjusting to all these green flags Cam was waving in front of my eyes, after all the fuckboys I'd been with. "Sure. Then I think I can handle monogamy."

"Your turn," Cam said. "What do you expect from me?"

There was a slight smile that made its way on my lips. "Business or pleasure?"

"Pleasure." He smirked and side-glanced my way. "Always pleasure."

"As you probably already know, I don't handle vanilla well."

"Yes, I gathered that much already. And I happen to love that part of you, so no problem there. Walk me through it slowly and we'll be alright." Cam turned to wink at me.

Heat creeped up my neck, so I turned to look at the road instead of Cam. "And while I'm not as big on the whole monogamy thing as you are, I still don't handle cheating well either."

"Noted."

"I guess that's it."

"Then how about business-wise? Just note that I'm still only a producer on paper, and not like the actual boss. That would be my *Papá*. At least until I get him to retire."

Again with the mysterious older Ortega. "What's he like, then?"

"He's pretty chill, a lonely old man," Cam said. "You'll get along with him, I'm sure. Big on business—he probably likes money more than me. How about your family?"

I shrugged. "You've already met Jemma."

"And your parents?"

"Ran for the hills once they learned I wanted tits of my own instead of a girlfriend."

"Wow. That sucks."

"Tell me about it." I pushed my sunglasses up my nose to hide the sting that was making my eyes water even after all these years. "I've been doing great on my own though."

"Their loss, then."

"Yeah, but I'm over it. It was a long time ago."

"Good, because you're amazing and you deserve the world," Cam said, and gave me another soft squeeze on my thigh. "You alright if we stop here for gas and snacks?"

I actually paid attention to the world outside for the first time in a while. Looked like we were reaching the outskirts of another town. Where did the time go?

"Sure," I said, and stretched out my stiffened back muscles.

Only a small while later Cam steered into the parking lot of this small mall with a gas station on the side. He filled up the tank before parking, and finally I got to straighten my legs a little after stepping out of the car. It was amazing—like my blood actually started circulating all over again.

My bladder also informed me I was going to have to face my mortal enemy, the bane of my existence: a public bathroom. It was still nerve wracking even though I mostly passed as a cis-woman these days, and men would look at me weird if I barged in theirs. Still, when I did use the ladies' room, I always had this annoyingly nagging feeling.

"I'm gonna visit the ladies room first," I said. "Let's meet at the café later?"

Cam picked through his pockets and handed me a spare key to the car.

"Sure, but take this just in case," he said, and started stretching his arms and back. "I feel like walking around the mall for a while. I swear after I turned 30, my body started breaking on me all on its own."

I grabbed my purse and shoved the keys in a side pocket. "Alright. See you soon."

Cam gave me a dismissive wave and I walked off.

Luckily, the whole short pitstop to the bathroom went well—there was literally no one else in it, so that might've been a factor. Relieved in all senses of the word, I headed to the small café I'd spotted earlier and ordered an iced caramel latte. It was wonderfully air conditioned, so I dared to pick a table right beside the huge windows.

I barely got one sip from my coffee, which tasted like heaven, before my phone started to ring. Figuring I'd be getting a call from Cam, maybe asking where I was, I answered without even glancing at the screen.

"Hello," I said, and took another sip of the cold, refreshing beverage.

"I'm away for what felt like one painful, baby puke filled minute, and you've resigned? What happened?"

Nearly spraying all the coffee out of my nose upon hearing a familiar female voice, I took a good look at the screen—only to confirm it was my ex-boss calling.

I pulled myself back together and muttered, "Hey Susan."

"Don't you 'hey Susan' me as if nothing happened. Spill. Now."

I cleared my throat. "So…do you want to hear the version I'm going to tell you in case I might want to work there again in the future when my new singing career flops, or do you want the version with all the tea?"

"Singing career?" Susan squealed. "That video—"

I cut her short. I'd still not quite forgotten that she'd shared it in the office's group chat. "Irrelevant. So, do you want the safe version or the version with all the tea?"

"Elle, you always have a job where I'm managing, and I'm not going to retire anytime soon with a mortgage whipping my ass." Her laughter rang, in that familiar way so I could almost imagine how she threw her head back like she always did when she was laughing from the bottom of her heart. "So, please, I want all the tea."

God, I missed her. I took another sip before replying though, because I needed to arrange my words perfectly. "Greg got on my nerves."

"I knew it," she said, emphasizing every syllable. "That bastard. What did he say, exactly?"

"He sprouted some transphobic nonsense about my voice when he saw that video. Like I remember the exact words."

"Did anyone else happen to hear that?"

I took a second to think. "I mean, probably the entire office did. I don't think the door was even closed."

"Brilliant. I mean, I'm sorry and you should've never had to go through that. But it was about damn time we got rid of Greg. I'm so going to get his ass fired once I get back to the office, and make sure he'll never get a job in—"

"Whoa-whoa, calm down." My heart was suddenly pounding in my chest. "I mean, do we have to take such drastic measures? Everything turned out great for me. I'm kind of not allowed to talk about details yet, but I'm in good hands. If anything, Greg's little outburst—"

"Oh, nonsense, I've wanted to get rid of him for years," Susan said. "He's already got himself a few warnings about sexual harassment and been moved from department to department every few months, but before we've never really caught him redhanded like this."

"It's your call I guess."

"Indeed it is," Susan said, and let out another laugh, but this time it sounded more than a little ominous. "Look, I need to get back to being a milk cow. Talk to you soon, okay? And good luck in the new career. Bye!"

"Sure. Thanks," I said, but the line was already silent, and I was left staring at the blank screen wondering what in the actual hell had just happened.

I'd still not wrapped my head around the call, when the phone vibrated in my hand. This time, it was Cam, but with a text.

Cam: Can you do me a favor? We should get going soon.
Me: Sure, what's up?
Cam: Can you get me a coffee to go and wait in the car?
Me: Alright. What kind?
Cam: Plain and black, I don't really care.

With a sigh I stood up, ordered Cam's coffee, and sorrowfully walked out of the nicely air conditioned small coffee shop.

I'd barely even gotten seated back in the passenger seat, before Cam crashed on the driver's seat, looking all kinds of jittery.

"Here," Cam said, and dropped a black paper bag with a huge red x on the side onto my lap. It was absolutely filled to the brim with stuff, and there was so much of it I had a hard time deciphering what the hell I was even looking at.

"What's this?" I asked.

"I happened to find an adult store," Cam said, and flashed me this huge, ear-to-ear grin. "Let's make this road trip more interesting, shall we?"

I studied the first still packaged item I could pull out from the jam-packed bag. "Nipple clamps?"

Cam pushed a button to fire up his over the top flashy car and carefully backed out from the parking spot. I quickly stuffed the nipple clamps back in the bag—people were staring at the car and the windows were only mildly tinted. I did not have a kink for public stuff.

"I still don't really know your preferences, so I bought a selection. You can start by picking out…hmm…let's say like three favorites."

"And then what?" I asked.

"I figured we could play this game called Simon Says," Cam explained. "Except it's really just Cameron Says and you don't get any turns to say."

When I stared at him, speechless, he added, "If you want to, of course. I mean, alternatively we can continue talking about the boring side of your new career as well."

I blinked, suddenly crashing back to reality after having been wondering how the hell I'd managed to get a guy like Cam to date me. He seemed so ready for stuff like this—and was putting his imagination to good use too. To think he'd said he'd always been vanilla before, because this was not vanilla behavior.

"No—I mean yeah." I took a deep breath. "Yes, I would very much like to play."

"Then pick something."

Immediately, I started rummaging through the bag, glad that we were already back on the highway and there was barely any possibility of anyone seeing what I was up to. There were a lot of items I found interesting, but I did end up picking the aforementioned nipple clamps, this small pink bullet vibrator and a bottle that said "warming libido glide," whatever that meant. I didn't pick them necessarily because they were the most interesting items of the bunch, far from it actually, but they looked enticing enough and would still be easy to use in the front seat.

I noticed Cam had also stopped at the gas station's grocery shop—well that, or the adult shop had also sold tissues and hand sanitizer. Looked like he'd really thought of everything, including the clean up. I grabbed some of those too and stuffed them in the glove compartment before opening the packages of the toys. Those I stuffed in the paper bag that I then put in the backseat.

"Alright, I'm ready," I said, laying the items on my lap.

"Do you have a bra on?" Cam asked.

"Nope," I said. "I didn't pay as much as I did for these tits only to make them suffer all the time."

Cam nodded. "Then take your panties off but leave the skirt on."

Heat crept up my neck at an alarming speed, but I did wiggle out of my panties before handing them to Cam, who stuffed them in his jeans pocket, a smirk flashing on his face. "Good. You'll get them back when we stop for dinner if you behave. Are you ready?"

"Yes," I breathed out, my heart already pounding incredibly hard in anticipation for what Cam had in store for me.

"Then, Simon says…"

QUEEN'S APPETITE

Elle's heavy breathing filled up the car and I regretted every second of this torturous game we'd played for hours already—but I was also addicted to it.

I was addicted to imagining her face. I said "imagining" because there was no way I could even glance her way without risking our lives. I was driving after all. Still, I bet she looked beautiful in her world of pleasure. I couldn't stop thinking about her flushed face, parted lips, and wandering hands that so readily obeyed every command that rolled off my tongue.

I was addicted to the way she said my name. She moaned it almost as if it was a prayer. It got more desperate each time she got closer to her release. I'd heard her go over the edge two times already, and I was adamant on making it happen for the third.

I was addicted to listening to her reactions. Tuning in to listen to every gasping breath, every hungry appeal to let her come, every rustling of her clothes. The way she became more brave, more daring after sunset.

"Cam, I can't hold it for much longer," she whined, the words causing a jolt of blood to rush straight to my already aching crotch. "Please…"

The navigator said it was only ten minutes until my planned dinner place. If I remembered correctly, North Point Bar & Grill had this dark, secluded in the woods and confusing parking lot behind the building. I was hoping there would be a nook in there where we could have some privacy—where I could watch Elle unravel. I'd missed it a couple of times already and I was not about to miss it again.

"Just a little while longer. You can do it. Close your eyes and breathe."

The whimper that escaped her lips almost made me nut in my pants. In all honesty, I was as close to losing it as she was.

"I can't, please, please let me come…"

"Hands off, Elle," I said, and saw from the corner of my eye that she instantly obeyed, the leg I saw quivering as she was holding back with all her might.

"Fuck," she mumbled, and slid her hands under her thighs.

"Good girl. You can do it. Breathe."

Realizing I was not going to make it all the way to the restaurant, I turned onto this small dirt road with the car, and drove until the asphalt road disappeared from my rearview mirror before parking to the side. A quick glance around told me we were quite literally in the middle of nowhere, only trees surrounding us. Good.

"What's going on? Where are we?" Elle said, and when I turned to look, she was staring outside, eyes all wide open and wild.

I let the back of my hand brush her flushed, heated cheek. "Did I tell you to open your eyes, *cariño*?"

Elle grimaced and instantly squeezed her eyes shut, leaning the back of her head on the headrest. "No…"

"Does this mean I should punish you?"

For a brief second, I got to witness Elle sinking her teeth into her bottom lip, before she breathed out a faint, "Yes?"

With a smile tugging the corner of my mouth up, I briefly let my eyes roam on her flustered body. It was trembling from all the exhilaration it had been through. It occurred to me; it was my doing. I did this to her. With my mere words and imagination, I'd somehow turned her into this quivering, writhing, panting mess.

The white, short button up did a very bad job hiding the nipple clamps or the chain that connected them to each other. Her hands were still trapped under her thighs, squeezing her breasts together so they were less than half an inch from falling off the shirt. Her denim skirt had rolled up and gathered on her waist, more or less exposing her privates, and causing her ass to sit in direct contact with the leather seat.

I'd never seen a hotter sight in my life.

She jolted as if she'd been hit by an electric shock when my hand landed on her thigh and started to wander.

"Oh, fuck," she muttered, then took in a sharp breath between her teeth.

"Still okay?" I asked,

"No—I mean yes," she breathed out. "Only somewhat touch deprived. You surprised me. So help me God because I'm going to come if your hand wanders up any further."

"God won't help you here," I said, my voice so low and strict I surprised even myself.

I watched her gulp nervously and slipped my wandering hand under her shirt and fondled with the nipple clamp trapped breast.

"I'm still mad you opened your eyes when you shouldn't have. I wonder whether the saleswoman was onto something…" I tugged at the chain, which caused Elle to raise her chest and let out a long moan. "…when she said it actually hurts more when you take them off than when they're on."

"She's right—" she started, but it was already too late.

I'd already yanked the left one off, and momentarily the interior of the car was filled with a howling, gut-wrenching cry. There was also an actual tear that escaped the corner of Elle's eye and rolled down her cheek. I never thought I'd be turned on by making a woman cry, but I would've lied if I didn't say I wasn't a second away from cumming my pants. It took everything in me to hold back.

"Shh," I hushed, brushing away the tear from her cheek and massaging the newly freed nipple back to life. "Everything's okay. We've got to get rid of the other one, too, right?"

Elle stiffened, and hissed between her teeth, "Do it."

This time, I made the sting last for a bit longer by first pulling the clamp off and then pinching the freed nipple between my fingers, hard. By the time I was done, Elle was a shaking, sobbing, broken pile of misery and lust all mixed together. I opened the front of my jeans to free my dick from its way too tight of a denim prison.

"Look at me," I said, and cupped the side of her neck.

Only barely opening her tear glistening eyes, she lolled her head to the side to face me—and I noticed she was actually smiling. And it was this slightly creepy half smile too, one that made it very clear to me that it wasn't actually me in charge here, but Elle. Her response to me more or less torturing her simultaneously scared me and made me fall for her even more.

I leaned in and reached out to her slick, hot, chewed up lips with mine, and her response was equally eager. My hand found its way into her hair and my teeth grazed her already swollen lips, making her moan into my mouth. My other hand reached under her skirt, causing another whine to roll down her lips when I graced her swollen, rock-hard dick.

We were both breathless when I ended the kiss and laid my forehead against hers. "Want to come together?"

Her nod was rather enthusiastic. "I want to taste you though."

"Then you've got to handle yourself, okay?" I said, and dug a condom out of my jeans' pocket before rolling it on. Then my hand fisted a bunch of hair in the back of her head. "And you're not allowed to come before I do, understood?"

"Understood," she said, and shook her hands a bit when she freed them from under her thighs.

I laid a quick peck on her lips before pulling her hair and forcing her head back.

"Open up, then," I said, and watched her comply before pushing her head down towards my lap without further warning.

She took almost my entire length into her mouth in one go, despite the position that looked very uncomfortable. I still kept her there until she gagged and convulsed in my hold, because she'd said she liked it. Not that I didn't—I had to close my eyes and lean back when the vibrations her moan caused a ripple down my cock all the way to my tightened balls.

When I yanked her head back up by her hair, she inhaled deeply, some drool pooling out and landing on my dick. "Oh, fuck, Cam, I'm going to—"

"Not yet," I said, and buried my cock back in her hot, wet mouth and raised my hips to reach a bit further in. "Good girls like you can hold on a little longer."

"Mmhm," she mumbled against my cock when I let her come up for a moment.

I took it as a yes and started fucking her mouth, ever so slowly. I was also going over the edge any minute. I could feel it in my aching balls. "Tell you what, I'm going to count down from ten, and then you can cum."

She bobbed her head and slid her hand under her skirt.

"Ten."

I pushed her head a little further down and continued my slow pace.

"Nine."

She sent another vibration down my dick with a moan.

"Eight."

I picked up the pace, my breath starting to drag.

"Seven."

Her hand movements under her skirt picked up too.

"Six."

My hand tightened the hold on her hair and my hips jerked, burying my cock deeper down her throat.

"Five."

Her small gag almost sent me over the edge.

"Four."

Miraculously, I managed to hold back.

"Three."

Oh, fuck.

"Two."

My cock started to pulse and my calves cramped from holding back.

"One."

I threw my head back, squeezing my eyes shut so tight it almost hurt. Pushing her head down, I came so hard into the condom that I almost passed out. Elle shook like a leaf on a windy fall night upon her own orgasm. Panting heavily, I let go of her hair and she straightened herself, before slumping against her seat.

"Fuck," she said, her breathing as ragged as mine was when she raised a hand that glimmered a bit in the darkness.

Completely on impulse and with an unexplainable need, I grabbed her wrist and licked off her clear, sweet cum. It tasted so good I moaned and let my eyes close. Her love juices were my new favorite flavor. "Why is it so sweet?"

"I see you're finally getting curious," she said.

"I can't help it. I'm fairly sure my cum doesn't taste like this. It surely doesn't look like this, so thin and clear."

"That's because you're not on HRT."

"HRT?"

"Hormone replacement therapy. I'm on a fairly low dose these days—there was a time when I couldn't come at all. I mean I had an orgasm, but nothing came out. It took me and my doctor a long time to find a good balance after I decided I was going to keep my dick in the first place. Are you disappointed?"

"About what?" I was confused.

"That I can't splatter all over the place like you do?"

"Why would I be?" I asked and sucked her index finger that had a bit more of the juice still glistening there. "I mean, it tastes awesome and is so uniquely you. How could I not love it?"

Elle pulled her hand back.

"You're making me all shy," she said, but I did spot a smile.

I pulled off the condom and tucked my dick back in my pants, then zipped up. "Shy and you don't fit in the same sentence." I started the car. "Come on, let's go eat something. You've made me hungry."

"And you've made me tired," Elle said, and yawned. "Um, so can I get my panties back now?"

I'd completely forgotten I had them in the first place. For a brief second, I considered keeping them like a complete pervert or a serial killer might keep a trophy, but eventually I caved and pulled them from my pocket.

"Thanks," Elle said, and started wiggling them on.

I tried to find a place to turn the car around, but that soon turned out to be unnecessary as I saw the familiar facade of the restaurant I'd been heading to anyway. The road led straight into the confusing parking lot.

After the pitch black darkness, with only the car's dim interior lights illuminating our little game, the bright lights of the restaurant made me squint my eyes. The closer we got, the more glaring they got. I parked the car pretty close to the entrance, but facing away from the lights.

I turned to look at Elle.

"We're here—" I started, but snapped my mouth shut as soon as I realized…

She'd fallen asleep.

She looked adorable in her slumber, arms crossed across her chest with her head leaning against the window, her lips all pouty and hair fallen on her face. I guess I'd really exhausted her to the core. With my chest aching with all the feels dwelling inside it, I reached over to the back seat and grabbed my leather jacket as silently as I possibly could. I draped it over her and quietly stepped out of the Bentley.

Making sure I locked the doors, I walked inside and ordered takeout. Monday was apparently a quiet night, because I got my order in like twenty minutes tops. When I got back to the car, Elle was still asleep.

I carefully laid our takeout containers on top of the dashboard and shook Elle's shoulder.

"Huh?" She mumbled and straightened her back. "Where are we?"

"Not far. I just found the restaurant. I got us some burgers and fries. I hope that's alright?"

"Very. I'm so fucking hungry," Elle said, and grabbed the nearest packet. "This mine?"

"Sure," I said, and grabbed the burger next to the one she'd taken.

She took a huge bite and groaned from the bottom of her chest, closing her eyes as she threw her head back.

"Sweet Jesus this is good," she said.

Gotta love a woman with a good appetite. "Yeah, it's my favorite grill in the whole world."

We ate in silence and Elle took the trash to the bin next to the front door of the restaurant, saying she wanted to straighten her legs. When she came back, she outright slumped on the front seat.

"So how much longer are we going to drive?" she asked.

"Only like 40 minutes or so." I started the car, then backed out of the parking spot. "You can sleep if you want, I'll wake you up when we arrive."

"Nah, I'll stay awake with you. It's not that much longer anymore," Elle said, but also yawned again.

I hid a smile, turned up the heat, and put on a radio station with relaxing music. It didn't take Elle more than a couple of minutes to start nodding off. She was out like a light after ten minutes.

With a completely idiotic grin plastered on my face, I drove the last stint of dwindling mountain road to my family's holiday home in comfortable silence. I was falling so hard for this woman it wasn't even funny anymore. Screw money, I would've slept under a bridge if it meant Elle could be happy and debut as a singer. I was completely serious when I said she deserved the world—I wasn't about to let her settle for less anyway.

Mi reina, I would've done everything for her.

Unfortunately, I couldn't, and with a heavy heart I admitted that it meant I couldn't treat this trip entirely as a honeymoon full of only love and steaming hot sex. I would have to make her put some actual work into making the album—and there was so much to do.

TEASER'S PREFERENCES

Based purely on the whole car ride experience, I thought we wouldn't actually get any work done. I was wrong. Cam had not only insisted we had our own bedrooms for the duration of the trip, but also very much put me to work, making me listen to what felt like hundreds of demos through the amazing sound system in the (main) living room of the mountain…residence.

I refused to call the place a cabin like Cam did, because it wasn't one. It was a whole four bedroom five bath mansion. I mean yeah, it was in the style of a modern log cabin, both the interior and exterior, but with, like, *a lot* of space and modern appliances.

I'd also analyzed all the songs Cam had made me listen to, because a simple yes or no wasn't enough for him. He wanted all the reasons for my rejections and acceptances.

"A learning opportunity," he'd said.

On the bright side, this meant we'd gotten the concept of my future album—yes, I was still freaking out about that—at least somewhat down in the course of one lousy week. There were even a couple of songs I'd grown attached to already. It was such a mindfuck to think that after they came out, people would associate me as the recording artist. It blew my mind.

I wondered… Would my songs be played on the radio? Would people actually come to see me sing, specifically? Would there be an opportunity to feature in someone else's—let's say for example, Gina's songs?

I'd never let myself dream like this ever before.

It still didn't make me any less irritated by the fact that my ears more or less bled from all the listening, and my brain was all mush by the end of the week. It was like the songs started blurring together, each of them only a slight variation of the others. It's not like they were all that similar, they just started to sound like they were. But Cam didn't care about my boredom at all, in his insane new obsession—finding me the hottest hit for next summer.

"No," I sighed, after another chorus that didn't make me feel any type of way. It was another cheerful preppy posh pop song. A total dime a dozen. Like, there was nothing wrong with it, it just didn't feel *mine.*

Cam leaned against his palm and played with a pen with his other hand. "I agree. But why?"

"Just…no. I don't really vibe with it."

"But *why* are you not vibing with it?"

"I don't know, Cam. I just don't," I whined, and slumped on top of the coffee table, so far I even accidentally banged my forehead against it. "Ow."

"Think about it," Cam said. "I'm trying to teach you here. 100% or nothing, remember?"

Rubbing my forehead, I pulled myself together and sat up straight. "Um, it doesn't fit the concept?"

"But it does," Cam countered. "It's sexy, upbeat and has a summery feel to it."

"Then, is it too mainstream?"

"It isn't, really, though. It's a brilliant mix of multiple subgenres, yes, but at the same time subgenres that are fairly unpopular as of now."

"So not mainstream enough?"

"Nah, it's got hit potential, for sure. It's sprinkled with clever lyrics that could make the song go viral, and it has this nostalgic feel to it."

"Ugh, I've got nothing. I just don't vibe with it." I started rubbing my temples. "A little help, please?"

"Hmm, let me think," Cam said, and twirled the pen. "Are we able to make the song sound like it's yours, specifically?"

I snapped my fingers. "It doesn't compliment my style."

"Now we're getting somewhere," Cam said, finally rewarding me with a smile. "The core of the song is too static, too flat for your range of tones. If you were a younger singer, we would gladly take this type of song so it doesn't put a strain on your still developing vocals but you know, your vocals are fully developed. We wouldn't be able to utilize the full potential of your voice without massive changes if we were to pick this song. Given to you, this would either end up sounding too flat or way too overdone."

I fell against the couch with a relieved breath. "Thank fuck."

"You know," Cam said, and gave my shoulder a reassuring squeeze. "I'm not grilling you just for fun."

"I know," I said, and closed my eyes. "But vibes are important, too. Business aside, I don't want to do an album and hate it afterwards, no matter how well it sells."

"That is true, but you still have to learn," Cam said. "At least to prove your point with better arguments. You're not always going to work with me."

"I know that too."

My heart sank. I'd actually done my research when I was waiting for this trip, and learned that Cam was a producer and composer with an incredibly high demand in the industry. On top of that, he took extra managerial roles within Ortega Records as the predicted successor of the entire music powerhouse the company was. He was wasting his extremely valuable time with a complete rookie like me, which made me feel like a pet project.

Which, in all honesty, I guess I was.

"Should we take the rest of the evening off?" Cam asked, pulling me back to earth from my internal downward spiraling.

"No," I said. I straightened my back once again and reached for the laptop to find the next song. "I can do it."

Cam grabbed my wrist mid-air. "But I can't. Come on, I still haven't even tested out the new hot tub they installed in the backyard since the last time I was here."

"But—"

"No buts. Art also needs rest."

"I didn't pack any bikinis though."

Cam pulled my wrist towards him in a way I ended up lying halfway on his lap. "Who cares? I've already seen literally everything there is to see and it's not like any outsiders are going to see us either unless they're hiking up the mountain and have binoculars. And even if there were, I'd say they've earned a bit of a view."

"True," I mumbled, as Cam started brushing my hair. To say it felt amazing would've been an understatement. No lie, I could've used a hot, relaxing bath.

"It's settled then," Cam said, and pulled me up from the couch. "Come on, you get the towels, I'll check the water temperature and get us some wine. Deal?"

"Deal," I said, but couldn't stop myself from first wrapping my hands around Cam's waist before laying my chin on his shoulder. I took a moment to breathe in his amazing natural scent. It was different here than in the city, somehow woodier. Or maybe it was the house. Not that it mattered, it was amazing anyway. "In a minute."

Cam chuckled, circled his hand around my shoulders and buried his face in my hair. "Take all the time you need."

I could've stayed there forever, but eventually the desire to try the hot tub won and I let go. Reluctantly, but I did. "See you in a few."

"See you," Cam said, gave me the shortest kiss in human history before turning me around and smacking my ass. "Go, before I take us to the bedroom instead."

As a giggle escaped from me, I admitted, "I wouldn't oppose that either."

"I know," Cam said, and winked, before disappearing through the door that led to the back yard.

With a stupid grin and feet feeling light as a feather, I all but skipped my way downstairs to the laundry room where the clean towels were stored, right next to the gym. Yes, the place also had a small private gym. Cam had taken advantage of it a lot during our stay, while making me work my ass off on the songs.

I'd grown to love the place. It was huge, but somehow had managed to keep a cozy feel to it. I wondered if I'd ever get the chance to come back here. It was still a little unbelievable to me that I was dating Cam, let alone getting absolutely spoiled by him.

I shook my head to get myself back to reality and picked up a few towels from the closet before heading back upstairs.

Cam was already seated in the huge hot tub, toying with his glass of red wine when I arrived on the terrace.

The wind hit my shoulders and I shivered. "Whoa, it's a bit chilly out here."

Cam turned to look at me, all relaxed, eyes drooping. "It's not chilly here. Come on, hop in before you freeze."

I laid the towels on the table and stepped beside the hot tub and tested out the water with my fingers. It was very warm. "Wow."

"See. Now get naked and come here."

Another shiver ran down my spine, but this time I wasn't sure if it was because of the chilly night wind or Cam's presence, or the way he ordered me around probably without even realizing what it did to me. Nevertheless, I glanced around, but realized I couldn't see shit because it was so dark. There wasn't much to see other than woods and mountains anyway. I got rid of my clothes in record time.

The water felt even hotter after exposing myself buck naked to the chilly early fall Northern California air. The water sloshed around because of my hurry to get my entire body under the water, away from the cold. But once I was there, and the water settled and I got used to the temperature, I was convinced I'd entered heaven. Even the stars reflected from the surface, making it seem like we were floating in the actual sky.

"Oh my God I needed this," I sighed, leaning my head back against the side of the huge tub.

"It's amazing. I want one of these in my LA house as well. Do you think I could fit one next to the pool somehow?"

Momentarily, I forgot Cam was rich and asked, like a complete stupid person, "Ain't these things kind of pricey?"

"Yeah, but you're going to make me lots of money soon," Cam said, and smirked. "Which reminds me, I think we need a different approach."

"To what?" I asked, then closed my eyes and slumped a little further in the water.

"To shopping songs. How would you feel if we tried to write you a song? That way, it would definitely be designed for you."

Reluctantly, I opened my eyes a sliver. "I thought we weren't working tonight anymore."

"You're right," Cam said, and smiled, then handed me a wine glass already filled with what must've been very pricey red wine—it tasted like a liquified orgasm.

But Cam kind of had a point. If we weren't going to find the perfect song, we should make it from scratch. The only problem was me and my inability to even think of where to start when it came to songwriting. However, the perfect topic came to mind like lightning.

"If I knew how to write songs, I'd write one of these moments." I said, and took another sip of the wine. "Well, trips like these in general, but especially about this moment."

"Interesting. Tell me more," He said, and his ankle brushed against mine under the water which sent an electric jolt up my leg.

"I don't know," I said, closing my eyes and giving a good thought to what made this moment so special. "Something about a road trip, being good with wherever the road leads or down with whatever activity… Bathing in the moonlight, naked, in the mountains, sipping wine that tastes like orgasms… Something cheesy like that."

When Cam didn't reply, I cracked one of my eyes open for a bit to see what was going on. Cam was staring at me, eyes on fire.

"Come here," he said, once our gazes properly met.

I only frowned, not wanting to move. "Why?"

"Did I stutter?" Cam said, his voice turning more demanding.

Now that, I liked. The tone of voice that promised me more than business talk. I still took my time, moving in slow motion. I wanted him to lose patience and manhandle me. To throw me around like a used toy. To my disappointment, he never did. He only wrapped his hands around my waist when I'd already reached him.

He turned me around and seated me between his legs. Pressed against his slick chest, suddenly I was not mad at him at all. His chest was warm, firm and comfortable against my back, as if I was meant to be there in his embrace. His lips landed on the nook of my neck and I melted, a sigh rolling down my lips.

"Enough business talk," Cam murmured against my skin. "Tell me more of your kinky little fantasies."

A smile made its way to my lips as I closed my eyes to focus on the sensations Cam's hands were sending rippling through my body wherever he touched. "Why don't you tell me yours? Don't you have any fantasies at all?"

"Not ones like yours. I'm new to this, remember," he whispered. "My fantasies are boring."

"Then you're a natural at it," I said, letting my head drop back to lay on his shoulder. "Based on the things you made me do in the car, I can't possibly believe you lack imagination. Any toys in particular you'd want to try out of the bunch you bought?"

Cam's hand slid across my chest, only briefly pausing to tease one of my erect nipples. "Honestly, I don't even know what half of them do, apart from the brief descriptions I got from the saleswoman. The whip with multiple strands of leather sure scares me."

"The flogger?" I held off a laugh because I didn't want to make Cam feel ridiculous talking about this. These things were important to talk through, I guess. "Sure, though I personally think it looks scarier than it actually is."

"Really? Then was there anything in that bag that you would be scared off?"

"Not really," I said, then gave it a more thorough thought. "I mean, there was this one kind of big plug with some kind of moving marble thing at the base, that could potentially hurt a bit…but with proper preparation, I bet I could do that too just fine."

"Now you've made me curious; is there anything you wouldn't approve of?"

"Oh, plenty."

"Like what?"

"For starters, I'm not huge on bodily fluids. I mean like spit and sperm is fine, but when it comes to things like blood, vomit, piss or excrement, I'm out."

Cam's entire body stiffened behind me. "Wait, people play with those too? I mean, no offense…"

"Some certainly do, I said. "Just not me."

"Wow. But wait, I thought you liked, you know, when I— um…"

"When you fuck my throat to the point of gagging?"

"Yes."

"I do. But I would totally tap out before it became worse."

Cam relaxed again, his wandering hands resuming their exploration of my body. "That's actually good to know. I can stop panicking about that. Anything else?"

I started counting with my fingers. "No breath play, choking, knives… Oh, and I don't want anything bigger than, let's say, an average porn star sized dick inside me. Especially without proper stretching."

"Got it," Cam said, and laid his chin on my shoulder.

"And above all: *no tickling.*"

"Mmhm," Cam said, and laid a soft kiss on the side of my neck. "No tickling."

"I guess that's it, for now. Anything you'd like to add?"

"I don't even know half the kinks that exist, apparently," Cam sighed. "Quite frankly, I don't know. Should I do some research?"

"We can figure things out as we go, too," I said, and decided to lighten the mood. "Anything you've particularly liked so far?"

"Everything," Cam said. "I've liked everything we've done so far."

I splashed some water on his face. "Specifically, please."

It made him chuckle. "No, for real. I've really liked everything. A lot."

"I really can't get anything out of you, now can I?"

"Fine. I'll tell you what I've liked," Cam said, and grabbed a tighter hold of me. "I like the way you respond to my touch with such eagerness."

He started sprinkling kisses on my shoulders, down my neck, each one of them making my heart start to beat faster and faster. A shudder made its way down my spine.

Distracting. "Mhmm, anything else?"

"I like the sounds you make when I play with these," he continued, then took both of my nipples between his fingers and pinched them. Hard.

I took a sharp breath upon the sting. "Cam…"

"And that…" Cam murmured directly in my ear, his husky voice igniting the fire within me. "…that I like the most. The way my name rolls off your lips when you're hurt, or when you beg."

The water sloshed around when I turned to face him in my sudden arousal.

"Then make me," I said, and watched in awe as his eyes darkened with the promise of absolute bliss. "Make me beg for it, Cam."

SIREN'S SONG

There was usually this gnawing feeling of indifference when I'd been with women before. I'd thought I wasn't the passionate type. But Elle… She lit this fire inside me, one that never seemed to diminish but rather grew the more I spent time with her. Not only in bed either. Even the most mundane tasks—be it filling up the dishwasher or taking out the trash—when I did them with her, it only made me yearn for more. It was just a different kind of fire, a smoldering one.

Watching her writhe on top of the bed, completely naked, testing out how much she was able to move—not much, by the way—with her leather-cuffed wrists and ankles attached to each other with short chains, was not that aforementioned smoldering kind of fire. It was the scorching hot, all-consuming kind of fire. The kind that held all the potential to make me do very questionable things to her if she as much as hinted she'd enjoy it.

It was my personal hell on earth. A hell that Elle herself had designed, just for me, by walking me upstairs, pushing me right into her room to sit on her bed with only a towel wrapped around my waist, and emptying our entire collection of toys beside me. She'd also already unpacked them, I noticed.

"Use them on me," she'd said, then dropped her own towel on the floor before chaining herself up all on her own. "I'll be your test subject tonight. Let's find out some of your kinks."

After that, there'd been nothing much I could do but watch helplessly while she got herself trapped, all her best bits exposed and on display for me.

"Is this alright?" Elle asked, snapping me right back to the present.

"You're asking me?" I forced my eyes up from her perfectly round, heavy tits, to meet her eyes. "I'm not the one practically immobile on the bed."

"Oh, right…" she said, suddenly avoiding my eyes. A blush instantly colored her cheeks rosy red.

Wasn't it way too late to get shy? It honestly looked like she only now realized what kind of position she was in. "Are you alright?"

"Yeah…more than fine, actually."

"Question: are you still able to roll over?"

"I guess so. Why?"

"I'm curious," I lied. In all actuality I was consumed by this unexplainable want to see her struggle. "Humor me."

"No," Elle said, her eyes sparkling with something I hadn't seen before. Was it…a dare? "Make me."

One of my eyebrows raised automatically at the challenge. Gone was the readily obeying woman from before. I was not at all sure if I was up for this particular challenge—it went against everything *Mamá* had taught me about treating women.

Then again, who was I to not respect Elle's own wishes. I guess indulging in her fantasies and respecting her kinks was also treating her right.

"This is really how you want to play, huh?" I asked, reaching for her thigh.

Elle's response was to snap her thighs together and flinch away from my reach. "Only if you're up for it," she said, her eyes burning with an almost threatening level of intensity. "Are you, Cam? Do you think you have what it takes?"

My hand stopped mid-air, shaking. The way her words sent a pulse of arousal rippling through my body, charging up every nerve fiber to a heightened sensitivity, and sending blood flow in a certain direction, conflicted greatly with my brain. It screamed at me to stop this nonsense. She was like a siren to me, luring me into deep dark waters with her challenge, her song, that was made of promises and laced with temptation.

My last warning came out almost as a groan. "Don't test me like this, Elle."

She squinted her eyes at me and smiled. "*Or what?*"

Her words all but evaporated the last of my resistance and the demon inside me stirred to life. In a feverish haze, I found my body acting before my mind could catch up. Ripping the towel off my waist, I swung it around Elle's knees. She yelped when I pulled the towel in such a way that she fell to her side. From where it was fairly easy for me to roll her all the way over to her stomach. The chains clinked when they tightened again and forced Elle in a bow-like position. She was so easy to control when chained like this.

"Or face the consequences, *mi sirena*." I grabbed her hair in a tight fist and yanked her face up from the pillow. A wicked smirk spread on her lips.

"Now we're getting somewhere," she said, her eyes already drooping.

"Be careful what you wish for," I countered and pulled her hair harder. Her back arched until her smile turned into a grimace. "What, isn't this exactly what you wanted? Any regrets?"

"Hardly," she hissed through her gritted teeth. "Bring it on, fucker."

Her entire body jerked when my hand made a rather hard contact with her ass cheek, before sliding up her spinal dip and over her shoulder, to stop on her flushed, soft lips.

"You already know what to do, open up," I said, only to get spat on my hand as her face turned away.

She was really starting to get on my nerves. *Fine.* If this was really how she wanted to proceed, I'd have to trust her to tell me to stop if I came onto her too hard. I took a deep breath to tame the fire inside me and let the calmness settle before tightening my grip on her hair and making her face me again.

I wiped her own spit on her cheek.

"When I say open up, you open your fucking mouth like a good slut should," I said, and pinched her cheeks in until she couldn't do much else than unlock her jaw.

"There you go, wasn't that hard now was it?" I asked, not waiting for a reply before pushing two fingers inside her hot and wet mouth. She gagged when my fingers reached far enough, making saliva pool in her mouth before spilling over from the corners of her lips.

"Good girl," I said, the words slipping out of my mouth without any effort whatsoever, my core glowing when I saw her eyes all hazed up from the praise.

Elle coughed a little when I let my fingers slip out of her mouth and I gave her neck a bit of a rest too by letting go of her hair as I reached for the toys. I didn't have to ponder for long on which one to use, as I spotted the toy that had interested me the most when I'd visited the adult shop on our way here. It was this black medium sized plug with a pink crystal at the end that also acted as a button—a click for each of the seven different vibrations, at least according to the brief manual on the back of the box.

I reached for it and tested it out. Worked as promised. Good to know it was already charged. This Elle…she really thought of everything. How long had she planned to seduce me like this? A day? Two? This entire week?

Meanwhile, Elle had turned her body in the restraints as much as she could. Her eyes were wide as she tried to see what I was up to, her breathing still heavy. I turned the vibration off and shoved the toy inside her mouth before she could start questioning me.

"That ought to keep you quiet for a while." I said. "Now make it wet, because it's going up your ass next."

Elle mumbled something unintelligible through the toy.

I smiled at her, satisfied with the toy's unexpected but appreciated silencing feature. "Same rules as with my dick in your mouth: shake your head if you want it out."

Not even an eyelash moved, that's how rigidly still Elle became. She might as well have yelled her consent, that's how loud her reaction to my little rule was. I pushed her lower back and forced her to lay her stomach fully against the mattress again.

"I thought so," I said, and made myself comfortable in between her legs, grabbing the lube amidst the toys.

The first drop made Elle shudder a little, but I made sure I lathered more than enough of it around her anus before working my index finger inside the tight, warm, hole. It made her whimper at first, struggling against the restraint, but once she got used to the feeling the whimpering turned into moans very quickly. I didn't have much trouble working another finger inside.

I made sure she was all warmed up and panting heavily, before reaching over and pulling the toy out of her mouth.

"Still alright?" I asked, only getting a brief nod as a reply as she dragged in breaths.

"With words, Elle," I said, and started teasing her entrance with the plug. "Otherwise you're not getting this inside and we're going to stop and go to sleep."

"No—I mean yes, I'm good," she breathed. "'No' for sleeping. 'Yes' for I'm good. Please, Cam, I—"

I cut her off by pushing the tip of the toy in. It was quite a lot larger than my two fingers, so I didn't want to rush it. "Can you take it?"

"Yes," Elle said, and moaned when I pushed it in a little more.

Once I got it past the widest part, the rest slid in almost on its own, and Elle took it all like a champion. I turned it on on the lowest setting, which made Elle spasm and whine out a small moan. So beautiful, an absolute pleasure to my ears.

I let her whine and writhe with the toy in her ass for a bit, before standing up and circling around the wide bed. She was so incredibly gorgeous in her lustful, euphoric state.

Grabbing her arm above the elbow, I dragged her sideways on the bed, so that her head hung over the edge of the bed. She knew instantly what I was after when I stepped in front of her, rolling on a condom—without a word, she reached for my half-erected cock with her mouth. So eager, so ready, such a slick tongue. I brushed her hair back, off her face, which rewarded me with even more enthusiasm. "What, not so feisty anymore are we?"

"Mhmm," she hummed, pressing her face on my heavy balls, not even bothering with words as she worshiped them with her lips and tongue.

It didn't take Elle long at all to get my cock standing tall and firm, ready to be rammed down her throat. But before that, I reached above her to give the toy in her ass a little boost, earning me a whole desperate whine from her. I cupped her chin and lifted her face enough for her gaze to meet mine.

Once our eyes met, Elle opened her mouth as wide as she could.

With my cock aching, I didn't need any more reassurance of her willingness to participate—it was as clear as day. I couldn't believe I'd ever doubted that in the first place.

Deciding to finally embrace my own primitive urges, I grabbed the base of my shaft and guided my cock in Elle's warm mouth. I let her do her magic with her tongue first, before sliding my hands through her hair and pressing further. My toes curled from the wave of pleasure the tightness of the back of her mouth sent through my cock and down my legs.

"Ah, you take it so good," I said, my voice at once turned husky.

I pulled back, gave her a second to breathe and pushed back in, not quite making her choke on it. I enjoyed the power trip. A power trip she granted me with her own excitement. It actually wasn't forced in any way, if you really thought about it. In a way, even now, with her restrained and at my mercy, it was actually her that was in charge. She had all the tools and all the words to get out of the situation or direct it to another way, yet she didn't.

Yes, it was Elle who was in charge here despite the way things looked.

That thought was more liberating than anything I'd ever experienced in my life, and sent me right into dancing at the edge of an orgasm. I rammed my cock as far as it could go, so far it made her mouth salivate enough for some of it to drip on my toes and for her throat to convulse as she fought back the gag reflex.

Pulling all the way out, just in time to not go over the edge, I held Elle's head up until her gags and coughs eased.

It was time to stop the games. I couldn't take it anymore. I wanted to become one with Elle, to bury my cock in her so hard I'd make her scream my name in that addicting way she did it.

She gasped when I turned her over, eyes widening in surprise. Pulling her knees apart, I bent them, then settled in between her legs.

I sent her right back to bliss by lathering her dick with a new layer of lube and turning the toy in her ass to the highest level.

"I want to fuck you so hard you'll be screaming my name," I said, pulling the toy halfway out before pushing it right back in.

"Cam…" Elle whined, her dick starting to leak with the sweet, *sweet* love juice I'd already grown to love.

"I want to hurt you until you're begging me to stop."

I cupped her breast with the hand that wasn't busy on her penis and twisted her nipple until a small cry rolled from her beautiful lips and a lonely tear stuck on her eyelashes.

"But above all, I want to take you through so much pleasure…" I pushed the vibrating plug inside as far as it went. "…you'll see stars."

"Cam—" she cried, so out of it she didn't even realize I had changed my condom and released the chains from her wrists.

So she yelped when I pulled the toy off, tossed it to the side, grabbed her wrists and pinned her hands above her head.

"Look at me," I ordered, satisfaction seeping through my veins when she obeyed instantly, forcing her heavy lids up. "I want to see your beautiful face when you come."

I buried my cock inside her with one prompt thrust, earning a long, continuous wail.

"But I'm already—" She gasped when I plunged in again. "I'm already—" Her eyes fluttered, but didn't close all the way. "—there."

Bewildered, I glanced down and sure enough, she was already leaking a small pond of that love nectar on her abdomen. Not able to resist the urge, I slid my fingers through the slick substance and almost passed out when I got to taste it again. It was surely becoming my favorite flavor of all time. I wondered…

"Then, let's see how much more you can take," I grunted and took a better hold of her, before starting to rail her right into the mattress with all I had in me.

With a moan, she squeezed her eyes shut and bit her lip.

"No, don't you remember what I asked?" I grabbed her face. "Eyes up here."

It seemed to take a lot from her, but she did crack open her eyes a tiny bit. I brushed my thumb on her trapped lip, until she released it from her teeth's hold. I slid the finger in, and kept her mouth open too. She looked so stunningly pretty when she was losing it. She was chanting my name like a complicated conjuration, with whatever other words she was trying to form, all becoming contorted, unintelligible.

It was the most sacred song in the world.

MASTER'S PUNISHMENT

Waking up all sore from the previous night's activities put a smile on my face. That smile was only slightly diminished when I stretched out in the warm bed to notice that the other side was completely empty. I cracked one of my eyes open to confirm that it was, indeed, void of a certain male body, and let out a sigh. Then my day brightened again when I noticed a cup of coffee on the nightstand—to my surprise it was still warm.

I scooted upwards and took a sip. It tasted heavenly. I wasn't really a huge coffee enthusiast, but nothing beat a good piping hot cup first thing in the morning. Especially when I knew it was made to my taste by Cam; dark roast with only a little bit of milk and no sugar.

I was rapidly falling for the guy. Well, I guess I'd already fallen, to be exact. When I woke up enough to notice the soft guitar sound from the downstairs living room, the glow that settled in the pit of my stomach only confirmed it.

That other night a few days back, after our whole hot tub moment, I'd finally learned how to properly make Cam lose control in the sexiest of ways. We'd barely managed to get any more work done since. But the days went by at an alarming speed, and I knew we had to get back to it sooner rather than later.

With a yawn, I threw the duvet to the side and forced my body all the way up. After rubbing my eyes of the last bits of sleep, I retrieved the silky dressing gown I'd gotten from Takaki-san from the leather chair in the corner where I'd tossed it last night. Grabbing the coffee mug, I headed off to the upstairs lounge, down the iron-railed staircase, then padded softly across the hardwood floor, following the sound of the guitar and Cam humming under his breath to an unknown tune.

After rounding the corner, I saw him sitting cross-legged on the couch, all but surrounded by discarded papers, a pencil hanging loosely from his teeth, as his fingers danced on the strings of the guitar. For a good while, I just stood there, admiring the view that was colored with a warm glow cast by the fire in the fireplace, the beautiful scene only interrupted a couple of times by him writing a note or two in the so-far unwrinkled piece of paper on the coffee table.

Cam glanced up when he saw me tiptoeing closer.

"Good morning," he said, smiling, but his voice was all rough and raspy. Whether it was because it was still early in the morning or because he'd been humming to the unknown song, I had no idea, but the way he looked at me made my heart perform all kinds of flips and cartwheels inside my chest.

Ignoring the heat that rose up my neck and cheeks, I replied with a curt, "Good morning," of my own and sat next to him on the couch, before pointing at the closest piece of paper on the table, the one I'd seen him write on last. "What's this?"

Cam put down the guitar, wrapped his arms around me and pulled me flush against him.

"I was inspired this morning, so I came down to write for a while. I hope I didn't wake you up?" he asked, and his lips brushed against my forehead.

I couldn't stop myself from leaning my ear against his warm chest and listening to the steady beat of his heart.

"No, you didn't," I murmured, and closed my eyes to enjoy the moment.

Cam brushed my hair. "Do you want to hear it? It's close to the finish line anyway and it's for you so I could use some feedback."

"Sure," I said, trying to scoot up but Cam pulled me right back to lean against his side.

"Stay right here," he said, and picked up the guitar, placing it strategically on his lap so that I could still stay close.

At first I imagined it would be harder for Cam to fret the notes with my whole weight against his shoulder, but soon forgot the poor man's discomfort as the song took me into its world entirely. It was very clearly written for me, almost making me scared of Cam knowing my inner thoughts that well only after knowing me for a few short weeks, the lyrics very cleverly dancing around my kinky side. Especially the lyrics of the chorus struck something within me:

Risky business, shadier the better
When I dance, I dance just for you
Tonight, tomorrow doesn't matter
I want to bring the freak out of you

The rhythm wasn't fast per se, it had some weight to it, but it wasn't a ballad either. If anything, I could've described the song as latin influenced R&B, pretty perfect for some alcohol or sex-induced late nights in the summer. More importantly, it was a song that I could completely make my own. I could already hear it finished in my head, a perfect song for clubs and parties, but also for the bedroom.

It was all over way too soon.

"It's perfect," I whispered, the words coming out as merely as a breath.

Cam put down the guitar and lifted my face, then met me halfway for a passionate kiss. Gentle and loving, our lips started moving together to the song's beat that still lingered in the air, until Cam groaned against my lips before pulling me to sit on his lap without letting the kiss break once. I wrapped my arms around his neck and replied to his eagerness with equal intensity, pouring all my unspoken feelings into that embrace.

Eventually Cam pulled back, and brushed his hand through my hair, following the strands from my scalp all the way to my waist. He looked at me directly in the eyes, the look telling me more than any words could—it was like he was looking at me like I was the only woman on planet earth, but was also somewhat in pain.

"Elle, I think I'm—" Cam started, but I cut him off by pressing my index finger across his lips, because I knew exactly what he was about to say.

"Too soon," I said, but smiled briefly before hugging him tighter and resting my chin on his shoulder.

Cam chuckled. "So let me get this straight; you've been so open with all the kinky stuff but draw the line at a confession?"

"Of course," I said. "One is a matter of preference and the other is life-changing stuff."

Cam sighed, but replied with a calm, relaxed, "Alright, I'll wait until you're ready."

I nodded and we sat there for a good while, holding each other and listening to the crackle of the fire. Cam played with the ends of my hair on my back right above my waist. It was exactly where I wanted to be. I was so grateful he'd found me that one starry night in Jemma's wedding, and I never wanted to let go.

I wanted the moment to last for an eternity.

Cam's voice was quiet when he eventually broke the spell. "We should head back to LA soon, though."

"I know," I said, and straightened up.

"I can't finish this song here without any equipment…and quite honestly, you're a distraction. A very tempting distraction, too."

I smirked, and rolled my hips to grind against his half-hard bulge. "Who, me?"

At once, Cam's eyes flashed fire and he trapped my arms on top of my head and made me yelp in surprise by lifting me and making me crash to lay on my back against the couch.

As he leaned over me, pressing my hands against the couch, his intense stare made my stomach tighten.

"I'm warning you Elle, I'm going to have to punish you if you keep doing this every time we're supposed to work."

I narrowed my eyes at him, challenging him. "Don't threaten me with good times."

His hand dove straight under the thin, flimsy gown and found my nipple. I took in a sharp breath when he pinched it, hard. "Are you sure?"

Feeling heat concentrate between my legs, I breathed out a faint, "Y-yes," as my eyes fluttered shut.

"Then get up," Cam said, his hand and the heat and weight of his body disappearing, all at once. "We're going to have breakfast, and you're going to behave."

"What?" I mumbled, still halfway out of it until I scooted up and my eyes focused again, only to see Cam was already heading to the kitchen.

He glanced at me over his shoulder. "You heard me. No fun for you until you've been adequately nourished and worked on the music."

Goddammit. My teeth ground together when I pulled the all but fallen apart dressing gown back in place and strutted past Cam to the kitchen. He smacked my ass when I passed him and chuckled at my clearly annoyed demeanor.

Damn the man for knowing how to play me like this.

COUPLE'S PLANS

Back in LA, my little escape upstate with Elle became a memory fading faster than a fever dream.

I knew it was my own fault that she barely ever had time for me anymore. Considering she was busy with dance and singing lessons, and arranging her new schedule with Zoe, we'd only been able to sneak in like two whole dates after we came back. I still couldn't help but yearn for more. I always needed more.

Leaning over the mixing table, my eyes scanned the track list we'd ended up with for Elle—twelve songs of pure toe-curling bedroom music mixed with a couple of more upbeat summer songs that had the potential to become huge hits. A lot of them were mine, either from my catalog or that one song I'd come up with in the mountains, but the rest of them seemed to frequent another well-known name in the city of angels: Micah.

I wondered if I ought to have him co-produce the entire album with me. He cost a lot as a well-known independent producer, and it would be hard to convince him to work with a totally unknown artist, but it seemed worth a try the more I thought about it. I wanted Elle to work with other people than me anyway, to avoid the album becoming extremely biased and therefore a possible flop—and also to help with the productivity issues Elle and I seemed to face any time we were trying to work just the two of us.

A knock on the door interrupted me before I managed to come to a full conclusion, but I didn't mind as soon as I lifted my eyes up from the screen and saw the intruder waltzing through the door. Elle looked absolutely gorgeous as she always did, but this time barely clad in low-cut mini shorts and a white t-shirt that was tied in a knot above her bellybutton, with her long, blond ponytail bouncing as she walked over to me after closing the door behind her.

"Hey, how's it going?" Elle asked, her smile lighting up the entire room and my mood too.

"Great, how'd the vocal lesson go?" I asked and grabbed her to sit on my lap as soon as she was close enough.

"Fine, I guess, but I'm exhausted," Elle whined. But she looked nothing like tired as she circled her hands around my neck. Her eyes sparkled and everything. "I didn't know singing involved so much *breathing*."

"Haha, just wait for when they're training you for live performances and especially a tour. I've seen them make singers run and sing at the same time."

Elle's eyes widened. "What in the actual—"

I cut her off, my smile turning into a smirk upon her horrified expression. "Listen, I'm glad you're here. I've been going through the potential track list and noticed we picked quite a lot of Micah's tracks. How would you feel if I'd ask him to co-produce this entire thing?"

"Hmm… I have no idea who he is, but I'm down with whatever you deem fit," Elle said, and shrugged. "It's not like I know anyone yet. Play me one of his tracks?"

I nodded, quickly pulling up one of the tracks and hit play.

"Oh, he made these ones!" Elle exclaimed and nodded enthusiastically. "I like the vibes, the energy. If he's even remotely nice to work with, I see no problem."

"I actually don't know," I said. "I've only rarely worked with him. You can ask Gina, though."

"He's worked with Gina?" Elle asked.

"A lot, actually."

"If he has worked with Gina, I'm down. I'm *soo* down."

I didn't like the apparent stab of jealousy in my chest but tried to not let the venom slip to my voice too much. "Don't you think your fangirling over Gina sometimes just goes a bit too far? I mean, you're technically colleagues now."

Elle's wide grin told me she'd caught me right away.

"What, are you jealous?" She actually went and literally *pinched* my cheek. "You poor little bean."

I grabbed her wrist, to detach her hand from my cheek, before pulling her closer so that our chests collided. Our faces were half an inch apart and Elle gasped in surprise with eyes widening. This time, she had vanilla scented lip balm. I could smell it. The scent almost made me faint on the spot. At least, it made me very light-headed.

"And what if I am?" I grumbled, the words heavy in the small space between us. "Huh? What are we going to do about it?"

"What *can* I do about it?" Elle whispered, her soft words tingling my lips. "The way I see it, that's your problem, not mine."

"Well," I started, and my hand traced the hem of her shorts, her thigh's heat feeling amazing against the sensitive tips of my fingers. "You could start by kissing me and see if that makes me feel any better."

Elle chewed her bottom lip, before replying. "And what if someone comes in and sees us? Wasn't our thing supposed to be a secret?"

"It doesn't have to be *that* secret. And do you really think sitting on my lap helps our case much anyway?" A chuckle escaped from me. "Believe it or not, I don't usually do this with Ortega artists. In fact, you're the very first."

"Ah, right." She sighed. "Then I guess it can't be helped."

"It really can't," I said, and closed my eyes in anticipation.

When Elle's soft, vanilla lips landed on mine, I was almost convinced I'd died and gone straight to heaven. Her kisses never got old. I realized I needed to be grateful for whatever crumbs I'd get from her these days, and planned on lingering in the kiss as long as I possibly could.

But her lips tried to part with mine way too soon, so I cupped her neck and brought them back on mine. I couldn't get enough. It was never enough.

Eventually, we did part, both breathless. Elle looked beautiful with her rosy cheeks. The tension slowly faded away and I cleared my throat.

"Are you free tonight?" I asked, my voice all hoarse already. "Let's have dinner and a sleepover?"

Elle's face fell and cast her eyes to the floor. "I'm sorry, Jemma wants to take me shopping and I already canceled on her once for dick, remember?"

To say I wasn't disappointed, would've been a huge fat lie. I laid my forehead on her shoulder, defeated. "Goddammit."

"And she thinks I don't look like enough of a superstar," Elle continued, ignoring my whining. "She's determined to become my personal stylist."

To my annoyance, Jemma did seem to keep tabs with fashion. I had personal experience of that, having bought her that bag for what seemed like forever ago. I sighed and straightened myself. "Getting one you trust, isn't actually a bad idea."

Elle nodded. "But if you're free tomorrow…"

My eyebrows drew together. Elle had been pretty adamant in reserving all Saturdays for Takaki-san until she'd be too busy in the future. "Isn't tomorrow Takaki-san's day?"

"It is," Elle started. "But I figured you could join us…if you want to, I mean."

Seeing Elle all roped up again in little to no clothes? "Hell yes."

That finally earned me one of those room-brightening smiles of Elle's. "It's settled then."

I gave her a small peck on the cheek before pushing her off my lap. "Now go before I drag you to my place and never let go."

"Again, don't tempt me with good times," Elle said, and winked, before escaping the way she came.

I slumped back on my chair, looking at the closed door behind her, already anticipating tomorrow's date at Takaki-san's studio. It was amazing how only with few words and close proximity, she made me fall for her more and more every day.

Sure, we couldn't see each other all day everyday anymore, but I was determined to make this work. For now, I was content to continue working on the album, knowing that I had the support of Elle, both musically and personally.

And who knew, maybe one day when I'd made her my wife and bickered about something stupid with her, I'd look back to this moment with longing.

What a scary yet alluring thought.

SAVIOR'S KNOWLEDGE

The absolute see-through, barely-there, light pink babydoll-style nightgown Jemma shoved at my face, made my ears turn hot. Look, I was good at kinky stuff, but shopping for lingerie, like, in person, was beneath me. I'd only ever ordered stuff online.

Gulping stiffly, I eyed the piece of skimpy, um…material…warily. "I still don't get why we're here when this shopping trip was supposed to be about my alleged superstar makeover."

"We already did that, and that was before I finally got to know about you and Cam," Jemma chirped, and started pushing me and my ever growing pile of shopping bags towards the changing cubicles. "Come on, at least try it on. Cam's going to love it. And you need to keep it interesting if you intend to keep him."

I scoffed. One would think I would be able to keep it interesting by means other than frilly lingerie. I mean, I guess it couldn't hurt to switch things up a little, even if it meant having to deal with vanilla, but… "I don't know."

My mumbled protest fell on deaf ears and ultimately, I let Jemma push me and my previous purchases inside one of the cubicles.

"I'll be waiting right here," she said, only offering me a quick smirk before dropping the garment in my already overfilled hands and yanking the curtain closed.

For a moment I just looked down, frozen and absolutely mortified.

"I can't hear any change of clothes business!" Jemma hollered, to which I sighed.

"Fine," I spat through my teeth and dropped my shopping bags.

I hung the scary garment on a rack and squirmed out of my t-shirt that by this time of the day, completely clung to my skin.

Not stopping to think for a second more, and especially careful to not glance at the mirror, I pulled the *thing* over my head and smoothed it out. It ended up being surprisingly comfortable and just my size. It still took me forever to lift my gaze from the floor to the mirror.

I mean, it *did* make my boobs look full and enticing. And pink always suited me anyway. It was just that the shape of it was grossly cute and frilly. Almost scarily so.

"Eh, I don't know," I wondered, unfortunately out loud, because Jemma took it as a sign to yank the curtain *all the way open.*

A screech left my lungs. "What the fuck are you doing?!"

Jemma's face was as blank and indifferent as she looked at me up and down. Then, a satisfied smile lit it up. "Looks good. We're taking it. In every color."

"Jemma—"

She ignored me and waved her hand dismissively, as she pulled the curtain back in place with the other. "Thank me later, I'll wait by the counter."

I turned my worried gaze back to the mirror. It *was* a nice piece of clothing and fit me and my figure perfectly. Defeated, I carefully changed back to my own clothes. Damn Jemma and her impulses. I was annoyed at myself for loving her still. Or sometimes even *because* of the impulses.

This was not one of those times.

Fine. I could buy a piece of frilly lingerie. No big deal.

First of all, complying was the best way to deal with Jemma. Second of all, I didn't *actually* have to wear the thing ever, if I didn't feel like it.

I gathered all my shopping bags in one hand and picked my new lingerie with the other, and shuffled out of the cubicle, hoping that this would be the last stop of the day. Shopping in person was *so much more exhausting* than online shopping.

At first I didn't see Jemma, but when I did spot her she was smiling brightly at me by the counter with a huge-ass shopping bag.

"Oh, you bought something too?" I asked, hauling me and my heavy being towards her.

"No, these are all for you," Jemma said, practically skipping through the shop to meet me and somehow managing to slip the bag somewhere within all the other bags I was already carrying. She then linked her elbow with mine and started dragging me outside. "Consider it a gift for finally ending your long as fuck single years. And the one you already tried on? I bought that too, there was another with the same size, so we can go straight to the next—"

The only thing my exhausted ears caught from Jemma's blabbering was the word "next," so I just had to cut her off. "Jemma, I don't think I can handle—"

"I thought I'd find you around here." A familiar voice cut me off in turn.

Hope of this endless shopping trip finally coming to a conclusion grew in my chest and I looked up to see a smiling Zoe leaning against her car that was parked by the road.

"Wife!" Jemma exclaimed and all but jumped into her arms. "What are you doing here boo?"

"I thought I'd come to rescue Elle," Zoe said, and winked at me. "You've been at this for quite a while, love."

"Nonsense. Elle doesn't need rescuing. Right, Elle?" Jemma said, but when she turned to look at me, I was already speed-walking towards the cab I spotted parked two cars down.

"Thanks, Zoe," I hollered at the same time I yanked the cab's door open. "I owe you one!"

"This one's for free," Zoe yelled back with a dismissive wave.

I crashed hard on the cab's backseat, interrupting the poor driver's dinner break it seemed. He looked at me with half of a burger in his hand and eyes wide as saucers.

"Uh, sorry," I mumbled. "I'll pay you double if you just get me out of here."

That seemed to have a bit more positive effect on the poor driver. I think I even spotted a smile.

"Sure thing, miss," he said, and put the burger down on the front passenger seat. "Where to?"

I told him my address and when the car finally moved, I leaned back, absolutely drained. I couldn't fully relax, yet, because I knew the way to my place wasn't that long—in normal circumstances I would've just walked. It was only my eagerness to get out and the fact that I was carrying a gazillion bags that had me opting for a cab this time over.

I wondered whether or not there was something actually useful in that bag Jemma had filled up for me from the lingerie shop. I highly doubted it. But I was intrigued to find out nevertheless.

"Sorry Miss, there seems to be some obstacles," the driver said, pulling me out of my daydreams, and I glanced outside to see there was a huge truck unloading furniture right in front of my building's door.

I sighed and gave the man a few bills. "I guess it can't be helped then. Keep the change."

Not that I was very thrilled about hauling all of the stuff, even for this very short distance, but it was my only option. I heaved myself up from the cab and started making my slow, tired way towards my door, starting to wave a hello at José who I spotted was helping with the move.

That's when someone's arm wrapped around my throat from behind and I gasped, instinctively dropping the bags, and grabbing the thick arm, my nails digging into the person's flesh.

Oh God this is it. I was getting robbed. I'd lived in downtown LA for over a year without a single hiccup despite the area's reputation, but of course as soon as I'd dropped my guard, living my dream life, something like this would happen.

"Evening, Miss Wright."

My blood froze when I heard that voice. A very familiar, annoyingly nasal voice that belonged to none other than Mr. Greg Montgomery himself.

When I got over the initial shock, it was already too late to do anything, even scream for help since he'd tightened his hold and started dragging me around the corner. His hold was tight enough for me to barely get a sliver of air in my lungs.

"Fuck…you…" I croaked, still. "Get off me."

All the reaction that got out of the man was for him to shove me hard against the wall and choke me.

"You really had to get me fired, bitch," he spat through his teeth, making me want to puke due to the small drops of saliva that landed on my face.

"You did that to yourself, bastard—" I started, my voice barely a whisper, but then my eyes landed on the glimmering metal object that appeared in my peripheral vision and then that was all I could focus on.

The fucker had a knife. I'd known the motherfucker was sick, but *this* sick?

"What, Elle Wright, tongue tied? Don't you have anything clever to say?" he asked and laughed.

The knife got closer, until it was right before my eyeball and turned into two blades in my eyes. I had to squeeze my eyes shut., I couldn't bear it anymore. How the fuck had I gotten myself in this situation?

"You know a trans-freak like you should be taught a lesson or two on how to please men—"

"I wouldn't do that if I were you." A deep, soothing voice cut him off.

José.

I opened my eyes just in time to see Greg swinging his knife towards him while still keeping me pinned at the wall. "Stay out of this!"

"I don't think I will," José said, and grabbed Greg's wrist effortlessly when he was about to swing it again. "I've already called the cops, too, by the way."

That seemed to freeze Greg. The seconds he contemplated what to do stretched into minutes in my head. Eventually his grip on my throat loosened and he scurried away like a scared animal while I crashed to my knees, coughing my lungs out.

"Are you okay, Miss Wright?" José asked and helped me up.

"How did he know where I live–" I felt silly as soon as I hissed that, this sort of breathy whisper the only sound my throat could produce. "Of course he knows where I live, he was my boss, I—" I scanned the surroundings, as if I even saw shit the way my eyes blurred and bounced around like some fucking ping pong balls. I squeezed them shut instead and grabbed my savior's elbow. "*José*... What if he comes back?"

"Shh it's okay," José said, and wrapped his huge arm around my shoulder and started guiding me back towards the main street and ultimately the entrance to my apartment building. "Let's go inside, shall we?"

All I could do was nod and follow his lead.

José sat me down in one of the armchairs in the lobby, knelt in front of me and engulfed my shaking hands in his warm ones. Huh. I hadn't even noticed they were shaking so hard.

"Do you need anything?" José asked, his brown puppy eyes filled with worry as he looked up at me. "Water? Soda? A Lawyer? Mrs. Martinez? *Mr. Ortega?* The police will be here soon and they'll probably want to question you at some point."

The back of my mouth was so dry I was surprised there was sound at all when I parted my lips to speak.

"Water will be fine, thanks," I croaked. "And..."

José smiled. "And I'll give a call to Mr. Ortega too."

I nodded, with a nervous, out of place and time chuckle escaping me as I evaded my doorman's all-knowing eyes.

DAMSEL'S INFLUENCE

When I barged in Elle's lobby, I was ready to go to war.

José hadn't said much more on the phone other than Elle had encountered his ex-boss and that the police were involved, but by the time I got my head wrapped around the gist of things I was ready for first-degree murder. I couldn't quite believe the turd Mr. Montgomery had laid his filthy fat fingers on *mi sol*, but unfortunately the state Elle was in—a complete wreck—testified that he had.

Yet, the police had their thumbs up their asses and hadn't even dispatched one unit to hunt down the guy.

On top of all that, the conversation between Elle and the imbecilic male officer she was talking with, was turning so unfruitful that it was downright offensive.

"Sorry, um, *ma'am*." The officer looked at Elle from head to toe before continuing. Funny how he didn't do that until he learned that Elle was trans. "There's nothing much we can do."

I'd had enough.

"So we're done here then?" I asked, directing the sternest gaze I could muster up on the spot, straight at the unsuspecting police officer.

The idiot winced and tried to mumble something about needing something from Elle still. However, I could see my woman was hysterically crying, exhausted, and *this* close to completely losing it, which meant she was my top priority.

"We're going." And that was final.

Elle nodded and I helped her up, weaving her arm through my elbow. José handed me Elle's shopping bags, the ones he'd managed to gather from outside. Elle wiped her eyes once again with the back of her hand, her eyes bloodshot and lashes a bit crusty looking.

I couldn't even begin to imagine what she was going through. The poor creature shook from head to toe. She was strong, though, the strongest woman I knew. We walked to the elevators in silence, wordlessly agreeing to go to her apartment. I had the feeling that she'd talked enough, given how aggressively the officers had interrogated her when I'd first arrived, so I didn't try to talk.

When we reached her apartment and the door closed behind us, her sorrow and shock turned into rage. I hated how little I could do for her other than be there for her when the gut-wrenching scream that had my stomach in a knot left her lungs.

She marched in her bedroom, kicked her shoes off and hopped on the bed, continuing to scream but this time into the pillow. I hated seeing her like this, but there was nothing much else for me to do than put the shopping bags down and follow her to bed.

Much to my surprise, once I was there, she completely curled up against me. The screaming stopped and turned into soft sobs. She trembled there for a while, as I tried to whisper whatever nonsense I made up on the spot in her ear to calm her down. It helped some, but I suspected that my fingers that ran up and down her spine had more of an impact.

Eventually, she fell asleep.

I caressed her hair for a long time. Until her breath evened out and the quivering stopped, and even after that for what must've been an hour. Until I was certain she was in a deep, deep slumber. Even then, I leaned back to check on her beautiful face and ran my thumb across her glistening bottom lip, before pulling my completely numb arm out from under her.

Thankfully she didn't so much as stir in her sleep when I scooted up and pulled the duvet better in place on top of her.

"I'll be right back, love," I whispered, placing a small kiss on her forehead, and walking into the living room.

I found myself by the window, thoughts scattered and rage burning inside me so hot it was hard to bear. The cityscape in its nightly twinkling form was not enough to distract me, however hard I tried to get lost in it.

My fists clenched into tight balls from the pure amount of self-restraint I had to endure so I wouldn't punch a hole through the wall. Sure, I'd been able to pretend to be calm when Elle needed me to, but as long as she was sound asleep I wasn't so sure I could hold myself together anymore.

It was all my fault. I had all the tools and all the resources to get rid of the bastard ages ago. I could've prevented this. I knew Mr. Montgomery was bad news the moment my assistant had compiled the file about Elle and mentioned him. Yet, I did nothing. I'd been so useless.

Then again… Could I have done anything, really?

I was too blinded by my desire to get Elle that I would've fucked everything up had I tried to intervene back then. So maybe it had been a good thing I hadn't intervened. However, after all was already said and done, there was little to nothing holding me back from using my slightly less than law-abiding contacts to get the bastard Montgomery *at least* six feet under—

"Couldn't sleep?" Elle said, her soft voice interrupting my murderous plans.

I guess I hadn't been as sneaky escaping the bedroom as I'd thought. Turning around, I faced her the exact reason to not indulge in my primitive urges. My woman, my sun, my queen. Elle.

She looked absolutely adorable, sleep in her eyes and the comforter wrapped around her shoulders like an oversized cape. Considering the circumstances, that is.

"Come here," I murmured.

My fists unclenched themselves and even the knot in the pit of my stomach loosened as I opened my arms to welcome her in my embrace. Smiling, the woman humored me, for once without any retorts, and I buried my face in her wildly tangled hair that smelled like comfort and clouds this time.

"Feeling any better?" I asked.

"No," Elle said, and I appreciated the honesty even if it made me feel awful for her. "But I think I'm getting there, as long as you don't leave. I don't want to be alone right now."

"I'm not going anywhere," I assured her.

"Good."

This whole thing made me realize that it was time to bury my highly independent decision making, and stop going to the extremes. I was no longer one lone entity; we were a unit of two. I had to take her into account before taking literally any action.

"I'd like to deal with Greg," I said, taking only a little bit of distance and looking into Elle's eyes that instantly turned wary. "And I'd like you to not spend too much time here until I've gotten rid of him."

That's when she squinted her eyes at me. "What do you mean by getting rid of him?"

"Murder." I was only half-joking.

Elle took a step back. "No."

"Prison, then?" I asked, following her. "A long enough sentence for him to never bother us again."

"You heard the police—there's not much they can do," Elle countered, pinching the bridge of her nose.

"I've got… contacts. And the guy surely ain't innocent either. I bet I can find something."

Elle looked at me, still looking all doubtful for a short while before finally muttering, "Sure. *If* you can pull it off, I'd like to see Greg gone. Just maybe not entirely offed."

"Good. Now for that other issue—Would you be entirely opposed to spending some time at Zoe and Jemma's place?" I thought for only a second whether or not to add the latter idea because we'd barely only just established our relationship, but ended up taking my chances. "Or better yet, at my place?"

To that, Elle sighed. "I mean, it's not like I'm really comfortable staying here either… I suppose Lola and I could do a few sleepovers at yours if that would be alright with you."

I bet the tips of her ears had turned slightly pink, but the place wasn't lit enough for me to see it. I couldn't resist the urge to cup her face and run my thumb across her soft cheek. "You, and your little furry friend, are the most welcome."

Elle fell back into my embrace. I buried my face in her hair.

Everything was back to as perfect as it could possibly be in this situation.

FAMILY'S APPROVAL

Life goes on. Life goes on even when you least expect it to go on. It goes on even when you just want to hide in your home and never leave. Somehow, that still ended up being the exact one thing I could no longer do.

I mean, I was way too busy to keep mulling over the whole incident with Greg, but I was still scared. I was scared to go home. I was scared to leave home. I'm telling you the scariest shit is when your *home* feels violated.

The most fucked up thing about it was that the police didn't give a single fuck about this so he was still out there, going to work and having a normal life. Unlike me. I'd been pretty much camping at Cam's place or Jemma's, well overstaying my welcome in each. I honestly just wanted to go home. I was *so* not ready to move in with Cam yet—we'd only known each other for a few weeks for crying out loud—and I didn't feel like staying at Jemma's for too long either. Mainly because it felt like I was third wheeling.

I just wanted my life back.

So I found myself knee deep in work. Especially inside the recording studio. First on our list was a new version of *Whisper*. *My* version of *Whisper*. Cam and I had made it even sexier up in the mountains.

The second time trying to record my version of *Whisper* was vastly different from the first spontaneous time I'd been alone with Cam. This time it was officially my first recording day as an Ortega Records artist. The studio was reserved for us for a few hours—and by us I meant me, Cam and my new main producer Micah—but at the rate people were popping in, I was surprised we got anything done. Yet, to be completely honest, I was only annoyed by it until it was Gina who popped their head through the door.

"Am I interrupting?" they asked.

"Not at all. We're mostly done," I said, and wasn't even lying…much. There were only a few bits Cam wanted to work on, but Zoe had barged in a second before I was supposed to start on that last stretch, insisting to get the recording process on video for some social media purposes or whatever. Cam had tried to argue at first, but it ended up with Zoe winning and Cam assisting her by putting up the camera on a tripod inside the booth.

I pointed to the couch next to me. "Want to join me for a bit while I wait?"

"Sure," they said, and crashed on the couch. "So you finally caved, huh? We're now coworkers?"

I scratched the back of my neck. It was still weird to me, to be working under the same roof with all these celebrities. It was even more fucked up for Gina, my idol, to call me a coworker. "Yeah, I guess…"

"Cool." They smacked my shoulder. "What are you recording? Already?"

"Ah, nothing of my own yet. Just a remix of *Whisper.*"

"*Whisper?*" They asked. "That's a huge song. Are you sure?"

"Cam thinks I can pull it off." I shrugged. "It was his idea."

The door cracked open again, and this time it was this older gentleman in a tailored suit.

"Carlos!" Gina called out and shot up to give the man an honest to God hug while I looked at them in awe. Why did everyone, like, hug each other and seemed to have no personal space whatsoever around here, I had no idea. It was like they were all closer than just work buddies, almost like a family. It was a very different atmosphere from the corporate world I'd been used to.

Also, Carlos? As in Carlos Ortega, aka Cam's dad, the big shot? I took a better look at the man and realized he was a total copy of Cam, but admittedly older. And had maybe like a shade or two darker hair. Suddenly my hands clammed up and I brushed them against my jeans before standing up too.

"I rarely see you here anymore. How have you been?" Gina continued once they'd separated.

"Good as always," he said, and turned his twinkling eyes at me. "Of course I had to come see what all the fuss was about."

I swallowed, hoping it cleared my suddenly restricted windpipe. "Hello."

"Hello there, beautiful," he said, and offered his hand for a handshake. "You must be the famous Elle everyone's talking about?"

I shook his hand. "I don't know about being famous, but yes, my name is Elle. Elle Wright. Nice to meet you."

"Get this, she's going to record a remix of *Whisper*," Gina said, and suddenly I wanted the earth to swallow me whole.

Luckily, Cam emerged from the recording booth just then with Zoe in tow.

"Papá! What are you doing here?" he asked.

"Apparently witnessing Elle here record a version of *Whisper*."

The way Cam gritted his teeth together was quite something to witness.

"No, you're not. Come on, everyone out," Cam said, and started outright shoving everyone through the door to the corridor, except Micah, Zoe and me. "Now."

"Come on Cameron, I wrote the song, don't I have the right to—" Carlos said, but was rudely ignored and pushed through the door just like everyone else.

"Don't forget to press play on the camera too!" Gina managed to holler through the door in time before Cam banged it shut.

He slumped against it and took a deep breath. Meanwhile Micah and I just looked at each other, the question evident in the air: What in the actual name of family drama had just happened?

"So, shall we?" Cam asked eventually, breaking the static in the air that kept us all jittery.

I was about to reply something along the lines of "sure," but something on the TV caught my eye—a very familiar looking building behind the reporter—SCRN Inc's headquarters. Unfortunately, the sound was muted.

"Can you turn that up real quick first?" I asked, and took a couple of steps closer, noticing it was the local news.

"—Mr. Greg Montgomery, a long time employee in SCRN Inc, was arrested from his work earlier today, facing serious charges of embezzlement amongst other—"

The screen showed a phone recorded video of the douchebag's tomato red face as he was escorted to the cop car. I stumbled back, my calves hitting the edge of the couch, and I fell on my ass. I hadn't noticed I'd held in a breath so I released it.

The biggest relief I'd ever felt in my life washed over me. A serene calmness that made my shoulders drop and my neck ache as if I'd been all tensed up for *days*. Which was probably true.

Cam sat next to me and took me in his embrace from the side.

"Are you okay?" he whispered in my ear in a soothing voice.

"How did this—" I started. Then a sneaking suspicion hit me. "It was you wasn't it? How did you know—" I paused. "You know what, maybe it's better if I don't know."

Cam smirked. "I told you I'd deal with him, didn't I? Let's just say I have connections."

I was about to faint. "Does this mean... I can go home, right?"

"If you want, yes," Cam said. "But *mi sol,* I'd rather keep you over at my place forever."

Tempting, but... "No. I want to go home."

Cam nodded and we fell silent, just staring at each other in the eyes. I halfway expected him to start persuading me intensely, but it never happened. I guess even Cam could be reasonable from time to time.

"Um, what's going on?" Micah asked, looking a little concerned as he watched the two of us randomly all chummy on the couch.

Embarrassed, I tried to scoot away a little. First of all, I'd forgotten we still had company. Also Micah wasn't supposed to know about Cam and I. Yet Cam held me close and didn't let me move an inch away.

"I'll tell you later," he said to Micah, and started softly stroking my back with calming motions. "Are you alright to continue the recording or should we continue some other day?" he asked, turning to face me again.

"Yeah," I sighed. I mean, if anything I was relieved. And a little curious of how it all went down in my last workplace. Though I was sure I was about to hear the rest of the story from Irene anyway. I grabbed my notes, getting a little nervous for entirely different reasons. "Should we get to it?"

"Sure," Cam said, shooting me with a questioning look, but muted the TV again.

I prepared myself mentally for the rest of the recording. This was the real deal, not only about proving Cam wrong. I also didn't want to make Carlos, who'd apparently written the original song, sorely disappointed in me, so that was a nice additional pressure. Ugh. Cam could've said something. Thankfully, I was mostly done already, except for the weirdest part. "You'll guide me through it?"

The thing is, Cam wanted me to record some super weird stuff to wrap this up. Like breaths. Humms. Hisses. And I was supposed to harmonize with myself. I'd been taking notes like crazy, but I still couldn't quite wrap my head around it.

"Of course," Cam reassured me. "It's only to finish up the thing, as otherwise it'll sound flat. Trust me, all songs you hear have this audio track on them."

"Okay then."

I took a deep breath and headed back to the booth with my notes in tow. I spread them all out on my sheet music stand, took a final look and pulled the headphones over my head. Without giving myself time to panic, I signaled to Cam and Micah I was good to go.

"Let's do the first chorus first, so you'll get used to it," Cam said through the mic that was somehow connected to my headphones.

It was a good idea, since the first chorus was probably the easiest, considering I only had to harmonize for a few bits here and there—none of that weird hissing and breathing stuff Cam had been teaching me. It was also still weird to hear my own singing voice—it sounded so different from what I normally heard inside my head. I guess I'd never really get used to it. But once I suffered through the cringe and got to the groove of things, it became easier to manage at least.

To my surprise, this weird breathing and harmonizing layer ended up being the absolute funniest to record. Once I got the hang of it and loosened up, I pretty much breezed through it with ease. I was worried for nothing.

No lie, it was a welcome distraction from the drama I almost managed to forget while we were recording.

Then before I even anticipated it, Micah said, "And that's a wrap right there. Good job, Elle!"

I pretty much slumped to sit on the bar stool for a moment, feeling like a deflated balloon. It took me a while to even grab the water bottle to take a sip to ease out my throat that felt as dry as sandpaper. Eventually, I collected myself together and scooped up the notes before heading back to the mixer room.

What I didn't anticipate was to see the room with lights off, and absolutely filled to the brim with people dancing or swaying to the beat of my version of *Whisper*, which was absolutely blasting through the sound system. Somehow, even Jemma was there, suddenly very much screaming at my face and shoving a glass of champagne in my hand.

I took a sip, while Jemma wrapped her hand around my shoulder to drag me towards the center. Eventually, the song ended and Cam hit pause so it wouldn't be blasting through the speakers again, then waited for a silence to set.

"So, what do you think?" Cam asked the crowd. "Did I hit a jackpot with Elle or what?"

That caused my neck to heat up from ultimate embarrassment and also a choir of opinions I couldn't quite make sense of filled the air when everyone was shouted on top of everyone else. The only one I did hear, was Jemma, because she was screaming, "I can't believe my best friend is a superstar," right into my ear.

It was only when Carlos Ortega himself stood up from the couch and raised his champagne glass, that everyone calmed down and shut up.

He cleared his throat. "To Elle, the first singer after Lizette herself to grasp the original essence of the song, while still managing to make it her own."

Another round of hollers filled the air, but I mockingly glanced at Cam with the most satisfied look I could possibly muster up from the spot. It only took that one look for him to bury his face in his hands and mutter, "True essence my ass."

With a content smile, I shifted my focus back to Carlos. "Thank you. I appreciate it."

"Welcome to the family, Elle," the older Mr. Ortega continued, and honest to God winked at me, the glint in his eyes quite the tell-tale sign that he meant it in other ways as well, which caused my breath to hitch to my throat. Had Cam told him about us? I guess he must've.

"Come on," Cam interrupted us, and started ushering everyone out all over again. "Doesn't anyone have any actual work to do around here?"

One by one, almost all of them filed out of the room, following Carlos's lead, leaving behind only Cam and I. Even Micah left, claiming that his work here was done for today. I slumped to the couch, leaned back, and closed my eyes, letting the tension and excitement finally take over my body.

"That was quite something," Cam said, and the couch dipped down next to me before hands circled around my shoulders to pull me into his embrace. "I think they're all in love with you already. So much competition."

A snicker left my mouth before I could stop it, and I glanced at him with contentment. "Cam, there's no competition."

He was smiling. "How come?"

"Because I only love you—" My eyes widened, and I slapped my hand on my lips. What had I done?

Cam's smile turned into a smirk as he pulled me to sit on his lap, facing him. "It's not too early for that anymore?"

Warmth flooding to my cheeks, I said, "No, it's still too early. I didn't mean to. It just slipped."

"Then let it slip more often, *mi sirena*," Cam said, and pulled me closer for a soft, brief kiss. "Because I love you too."

Siren's Crisis

Epilogue: 2 years later

Takaki-san stood in my way, in front of the door that led to Elle, calm and unwavering.

"Look, Takaki-san," I growled through my clenched teeth. "I swear to God if you don't move this instant—"

"Calm down first," Takaki-san said, his voice as steady and collected as ever. "You can't see the bride. Think of the traditions."

I took in a deep breath through my nose and closed my eyes for a brief few seconds, trying to force my hands to stop shaking by fisting them into tight balls.

"With all due respect, do you think I give a single shit about the traditions if my bride calls me audibly *sobbing* a whole ten minutes before I'm finally going to marry her? No, no I don't."

I fell into a staring contest with Takaki-san, and I studied the older man's deep brown eyes with similar intensity to him studying mine. I couldn't care less if he'd think less of me; I needed to get through to the other side of the door. I had a feeling Takaki-san didn't fully grasp what I'd had to go through to get to this point. I was *not* about to let Elle slip away or cancel the wedding or anything of the sort. It had taken me literal months—even longer than it took to get her to sign to Ortega Records—to get her to marry me, so whatever crisis she was having this time over would not postpone this godforsaken wedding for another minute.

It was truly funny how I, now officially the owner of *the* Ortega Records, had to go through such lengths just to get a woman to marry me. A *willing woman* at that, a woman who at least had said she loved me and everything.

"Cameron-san, you might not care about the traditions, but Elle does," Takaki-san eventually huffed, still staying put as if his feet were glued to the floor.

I was losing my patience all over again. "*Move,* or I'll move you out of the way myself and kick the entire door in if I have to."

Takaki-san sighed. "Look, I will. But you need to promise me you wont peek through the curtain they've set up to hide her. And *please* try to calm down too."

"I promise," I said, without a moment of hesitation. "I do. Now let me in, *please.*"

"Very well," he said, and finally moved aside, his stern expression turning into an old man's smirk. "And good luck. You're going to need it."

I didn't waste any more precious seconds at Takaki-san, and barged right inside the room Elle and her bridal team had occupied since early in the morning. Jemma was the first one I noticed, as she glanced at me when I entered, throwing her arms up.

"She's all yours," Jemma said, and ushered everyone out except Elle, whose quiet sobs I heard from the other side of the curtain that divided the room in two. "Try to make it quick. We need to fix that make-up before the ceremony too."

I nodded, then shook off the annoyance the best I could and forced my voice to smoothen out before I approached the curtain that separated me from the weeping love of my life.

"*Sirena...*" I started. "What's wrong?"

"It's so stupid," she said in between her sobs and then blew her nose. "It's nothing. I'll pull myself together. Go away."

I swallowed the sigh that was about to escape my lungs. "It's clearly not nothing, so please just say what's bothering you so I don't have to worry about you leaving me at the altar."

Elle chuckled, said, "We don't have an altar," and then burst into an even more hysterical crying fit. "You would have one if you were marrying an actual woman. I'm a fake. Can't even get married in a church let alone have children..." *Sob. Sneeze. Hiccup.* "If someone should leave it's you."

This time I was not as successful in keeping the sigh to myself. "Elle, we've been through this. I don't care about those things. Yes, I might be a former Catholic, but I don't need a church to marry you. We can adopt if you want kids. Now please tell me what's this all actually about?"

There was another hiccup on the other side of the curtain, and then the sobs slowly faded. Finally, Elle admitted, "I forgot the blue."

My eyebrows drew together. "Blue?"

"You know; 'something old, something new, something borrowed, something blue.' And I don't even have a garter but Jemma promised to get one somewhere before the tossing thing."

Ah. The traditions. Should've known.

"And Jemma couldn't figure the blue out?" I asked. This seemed more like a maid of honor territory.

"She forgot it too, until the makeup artist asked about it. We only got this ugly blue ribbon one of the bridesmaids happened to have. I can't possibly put it anywhere visible!"

"Does it need to be visible? Hang it from your underwear or something."

"I mean, I would..." Elle started, and I heard some rustling. "If I had any on."

"Damn you woman," I cursed through my teeth. This was the single most awkward time to get a hard on, yet I instantly felt all the blood start rushing to a certain direction. "Can you show me the ribbon so I can see if there's anything we can do with it?"

"Sure," Elle said, and this long, baby blue satin ribbon with white mini hearts printed on, slid to my feet from under the curtain.

Elle was right. It was hideous. More suitable for a baby shower than a goddamn wedding. But...an idea struck my brain, some kind of a miracle.

"Takaki-san," I hollered, guessing he'd never left his guard post.

Sure enough, the old man's head popped in through the crack of the door.

"Is something wrong, Cameron-san?"

I raised the blue ribbon from the floor.

"Can you make this into a garter?" I asked, then glanced at my wristwatch. "Within seven minutes?"

Takaki-san frowned and took a couple of careful steps inside the room. "You mean rope art?"

"Yeah."

"No, not in seven minutes," Takaki-san said, and took the ribbon out of my hands. "But in ten minutes, maybe. It's certainly long enough."

That was all the confirmation I needed. I turned to face the curtain again.

"Elle, does this work?" I asked.

There was a single sniff, before she spoke. "Yeah, I guess."

Suddenly, Jemma was back as well, and both Takaki-san and I turned to look at the woman standing in the open doorway. "Great. Now Cameron gets the hell out of here and Takaki-san, you're going to have to work on it while we're here. The makeup needs a retouch."

I threw my hands up in a sign of surrender and started to back off, until Elle interrupted us with a curt, "See you soon."

It brought a smile back to my face. "See you soon, love," I said, and headed out.

The first thing I did was to find Gina, who was lounging on the terrace of our mountain cabin. She was arranging notes on the stand of the grand piano which was hauled outside for the ceremony that was about to happen right next to the terrace, the wedding arch having an incredible backdrop of the mountain view.

The sight would've taken my breath away—I hadn't seen the whole set up yet, the ceremony decorations were Elle's doing—except I had more urgent things to do than marvel at the beautiful set up that was currently filling up with guests taking their seats.

I tapped Gina's shoulder. "Can you improvise and make the intro a little longer? We need to delay the start for like five minutes."

Gina looked at me all weird. "Why? Is something wrong?"

"No, nothing's wrong…" I hoped. "Just a minor bridal crisis."

To that, Gina chuckled. They'd also gotten their fair share of numerous Elle crises as the designated musician. "Sure."

That was when Zoe joined us.

"Well, crisis or not, *we* have to go Cam," she said, and started pushing me towards the crowd. "*We* need to be up there before the ceremony starts."

I flashed her a brief grin. She was my best man. Unconventional, but she was my best friend and I couldn't figure out a better person for the job. Besides, there'd been little to nothing conventional in the entire wedding of me and Elle anyway.

Except, of course, Aunt Becky, who had already started her coughing fit, sitting in the third row. It reminded me of the day I'd met Elle. I couldn't help but feel this glow in my chest and a stupid grin spread on my lips when I walked to stand up front.

The officiant walked to the center, and I nodded at him. After that, it was a whole waiting game. Gina started playing. And she played another piece. And another.

And another.

The few minutes I stood there, being stared at by the hundred or so guests, were the longest minutes of my entire life. The glow inside me diminished. The necktie started suffocating me. Gina also started to panic, and played the last piece she had, less than half the tempo it was supposed to be.

Just when I was losing all hope and rolled my weight from one foot to the other, I finally spotted the bridesmaids filing out of the mountain cabin. Behind them were Elle and Takaki-san—Elle being the most gorgeous bride to ever exist on planet earth with her white, lacy dress, and long hair framing her beautiful face in wild waves.

It only took a second for the nearly diminished glow inside me to turn into a full inferno of feelings, and at once when my eyes met Elle's who'd started to walk down the aisle, we were in our own little world.

It was safe to say I no longer detested weddings.

PLAYLIST

I'm Good (Blue)
David Guetta, Bebe Rexha

Red Lights
Stray Kids

Self Control
Bebe Rexha

BTBT
B.I, Soulja Boy, DeVita

God is a woman
Ariana Grande

Need to Know
Doja Cat

WANT
TAEMIN

S&M
Rihanna

Mmmh
KAI

Power
Little Mix

More From Nami

ON STAGE TRILOGY

It has been nearly three years since GRiD – the gayest K-pop boyband in history – last saw the limelight before serving their mandatory military service.

Now, they are making a comeback.

***

Minjae, the lead dancer of an idol group GRiD, wants to make sure that everything is perfect for their upcoming comeback, down to the tiniest details. Including and especially the all-important fanservice. The problem? Minjae hates fanservice. Especially the part where people expect Minjae and his bandmate Do-hyun to act as lovers.

Unfortunately, Minjae has a secret – he once fell for Do-hyun in real life. Swearing not to make the same mistake ever again, he decides to ignore his feelings for the time being.

What if the chemistry the two clearly have on stage starts to leak into real life as well?

ACKNOWLEDGEMENTS

Beta readers: I would never have gotten this done without you.

Also, extra special thanks for my online writing community on Discord—The Dumpster—for being a shoulder to cry on and for giving me all the encouragement in the world.

To my readers: I hope to see you all on my next projects as well, so please check out my website for the latest news:

www.namiartopit.com

As always, enjoy…
xoxo Nami